RENEW

WRITTEN BY:

TONYA BROWN RIVERS

Dear Reader,

I pray "Renewal" will warm your soul and enlighten your spirit... ♡

Blessings...

Sincerely,

Tonya

Nov. 2017

Editor: Artessa Michele
Book Cover: Elle Welch
Formatting by: Sheena Binkley
Published in the United States of America

Acknowledgments

But seek first His Kingdom and righteousness and all these things will be added unto you.

Matthew 6:33

First giving all Honor and Glory to my Lord and Savior, Jesus Christ…without him none of this would have been manifested. I would like to thank my supportive family and friends for they have been in my corner of this process.

Authors and literary supporters: Sheryl Lister, Rhonda McKnight, Michelle Kimbrough, J.L. Campbell, Barbara Joe Williams and Chanta Jefferson Rand…ladies you have been in my corner throughout this journey and I so appreciate the encouragement, support and nuggets of knowledge.

My husband, Mitchell and sons Kendall and Cameron Rivers, thank you so much for loving me and for unchanging support. You have stood by me the entire time! Love you, so much!

Thank you to my parents, Willie C. Brown, Jr. and Fannie A. Brown, I love you and thank you for providing me with the tools to write in my diaries, and journals those tools paid off! I Love you, so much for believing in me!

Thank you, to my brothers, Victor Brown Sr. and Anthony Brown; you're the best brothers, ever! Thank you, too for your unconditional love and support! Love you, much! And to my family and friends, too many to name, but you know I love you and your support means a lot! Brother in- laws, Gilbert, James and Paul Rivers, Sister in-laws, Cynthia Brown, Vickie Johnson Rivers and Sylvia Rivers thank you so much, love you, my sisters! My nephews, Victor Jr. Xavier Brown, Christopher and Demetri Rivers, Harrison and Chandler Rivers, and my great nephews, cousins, aunts, uncles… and I pray I'm not leaving anyone out— but all the love to my family and extended family members. Love you, all!

To my beta readers, who patiently read "countless of chapters during this journey.Maggie Johnson, Angela T. Hogan, Elnora Dixon, Nakila 'Nikki' Monteith, and my literary event sisters, who help to market me well! Montaye Strafford and Shekei Odoms. And then there are my literary research sisters, Shannon Warren and Angela Peele. Thank you all ladies for your supportive feedback! And to the rest of my fellow team members of Novant Health, Child Development Center, my extended family and my supportive link, thank you, as well!

And to my long-time dearest friend, Darlene Hyman thanks for the heart-felt years of unconditional sisterhood...

And to the readers...I pray you will be inspired... I would love to hear from you! Facebook Fan Page triversnovelist and the website for the novella: renewaltopassion.com

To Sheena Binkley, thank you for believing in me and my story...I appreciate your patience and support of allowing me to be as creative as I can be. You and your talented team are awesomely, great! I have enjoyed the journey bringing my story to the limelight and my dream, a reality! And to the fabulous and talented fellow authors of SBinkley, Liz Doss, Lynette Edwards, Tameka S. Brumsey and Alithea-Jae Smith, let's always give them something to "talk about" beyond the caption reading, THE END...

Biography photo: Photography By Orrj Sinclair, Cosmetologist and Hairstylist, Angela T. Hogan

Chapter 1

"Please tell me you can be civil and professional with Corliss?" Tanner Morris' exasperated tone zapped Gavin McCoy from his musings. He had been successful ignoring the scolding while sketching his innovative designs, but his best friend and publicist just put a monkey in that wrench when he mentioned her name. To say he was salty by it all would be an understatement; he was stone livid.

Throwing up his arms and letting them drop to his sides, Tanner tapped his foot expectantly while Gavin pouted, twisting his mouth wryly as a petulant child. This was not how he expected his day to turn out—a conversation about her. As far as he was concerned, the woman didn't exist in his life anymore and it was all her fault. End of story.

"Tell her to go away!" he huffed. His dark, chocolate-brown face matched the stoic mood he tried to convey, when he really wanted to yell his frustration from the mountain top.

"Really? Gav dude, come on already," Tanner sighed heavily. "Is this how you want to allow things to blow up in your face? Grow up, man!" he replied with a shake of his head.

Gavin grimaced, exhaling in a long breath. He prepared to ask the dreaded question that had his stomach knotted in a fiery ball, threatening an ulcer. "How long, Tanner? How long will I have to work with her?"

Tanner winced. Obviously annoyed by Gavin's cool reproach, he glared at his best friend of twenty-six years, "She has a name and…" he paused. Scratching his head, he blew out a wisp breath. "I know you're not going to like this but more like a season-"

"What the-" Gavin's words stalled in mid-sentence. He would not fly into a litany of cursing. He promised his mother he would work on bridling his tongue so, instead, he bit into his bottom lip, hard, and squeezed his eyes shut, only reopening them when he heard Tanner drone on.

"Look. Gavin, you've got to play it cool, man. I've got you, right?"

He sauntered over and clasped Gavin's shoulder, patting it lightly. "Let's ball, playa. Let's make it do what it do!"

Gavin chuckled low. Tanner was a Harvard graduate with a Master's degree in public relations. It was always intriguing to hear him trying to be hip when he was trying to drive a point home; in fact, Gavin always thought Tanner should've been an attorney. He knew how to plead his case and was doing a magnificent job convincing him, even if he had resulted to his brother man style of tactic.

His show of two seasons meant a lot to him. So, if he had to stomach being in her presence longer than he could handle, he would have to do it for the sake of increasing his ratings and popularity, for that matter. After all, it was all about the mighty dollar and the 'brand'. Gavin knew he was a hot commodity; great looks, stellar talent, and personality were all that had him at the top of his game as a celebrity interior designer, until he discovered some bad news, turning his life upside down and inside out.

Yes. He still had it, but the luster had faded in a slight dimming. Nothing he thought couldn't be resolved. And, besides, he didn't need her to come to his rescue. But his hands were tied, and Gavin had to be around Corliss Valencia Adams now, in a different light. Not to mention, he wasn't completely over her and a day didn't go by that he didn't at least think about how she was doing? Or that smile, the woman took his breath away. Literally.

Gavin was a glutton for punishment. Shaking his head furiously, he knew things were about to get complicated again, and he didn't need this right now. But, he didn't have a matter in the case. Innovative Designs Network was showing a decrease in ratings and the producers stayed in his ear about getting out the funk they said he was entrenched in for the last few months. Gavin halted his friend's words with a raise of his hand. "Chill T." He nodded.

"So, you good?"

Gavin shook his head vehemently. "No. Nah, man. I wouldn't say I'm all that, but business is business," he groused.

"Exactly! And personal is personal, so let's not confuse the two, aiight?" Amusement danced around in Gavin's dark onyx eyes. Tanner was trying to distract his sour mood; he wasn't slick. Momentarily, it was working, but then it hit him like a ton of bricks. She was back. He tried squelching the gut wrenching feeling that churned his stomach and stung his chest in a dull coil of pain, all reminders that he still loved her just as the day he laid all his inhibitions on the line and asked her to be his soul mate for life. There was no denying it. The connection was still there, drawing him in at a magnetic force too potent to ignore.

Gavin grounded out a menacing groan. His long torso sank further in the charcoal-gray wingback sofa. He reflected on all that took place before his regular morning jog. It now made sense. "Talk about having a 'you have got to be kidding me' kind of day," Gavin thought out loud. It was all about trepidation. He now knew why or, more importantly, whom.

This morning, he almost knocked himself unconscious slamming his skull into his Butler design kitchen cabinets; how many times had his mother Evangelist Gretchen Clarke McCoy warned him about those cupboards. She was always preaching functionality over innovation and, with Gavin at six-foot-three today, he agreed wholeheartedly with her logic.

His best friend since childhood and publicist, Tanner Morris, informed him that his syndicated TV hosting show, Gavin Makes House Calls with Home Designs Innovations, would be canceled this fall if viewing rates didn't pick up, and, now, the assault of all nuisances, Corliss, was back in town. And, this time, he was told she was here to stay.

***

"Are you sure you made the right decision to taking Gavin on as a client? I mean, we can haul it out of here like we breezed in. I'm fine with the return for job purposes, but I'm not relocating and staying my behind in Atlanta. Which reminds me, why are you moving back permanently? Do I have to remind you that you're a freelance image consultant and can reside wherever you want?" Caitlin Reynolds, Corliss Adam's cousin and personal assistant, implored. They were dining at one of their favorite Italian restaurants, Buca, for dinner.

Corliss chewed her lasagna thoughtfully, swallowing hard, before turning uncertain eyes at her. "That's if he agrees, Cay." Cay, she affectionately called her since she could remember. She was the youngest first cousin on her mother's side. "I have to admit when Tanner called to request our help in boosting sales for Gavin's show, I was more than hesitant but knew I wanted to support and, so, I'm back to do just that and nothing more. Trust, I know how irresistible Gavin can be. I love… I mean admire him and I'm proud of his accomplishments." Oops! She almost let that declaration slip. "So there, yes." She nodded, "I know what I'm doing and you don't have to worry about me. And for why I'm making Charlotte my home again is because I've been planning to return for over a year, remember? Don't worry, I won't allow myself to be hurt by him ever again. This is only business." *And only a test so help me Lord…*

Caitlin chuckled knowingly. "Right, and that's why you dragged me back here with you so fast, to convince me to move back, too." she smiled coquettishly, "knowing I would be tempted to say yes, so I could get all close and personal with Tanner. Whew! That man makes me want to-"

"Rein those cravings in girl." Corliss laughed heartily. "I need you focused and on board to saving the show, remember? Operation save Gavin?" Corliss arched a teasing eyebrow.

"And you have my allegiance, but a girl got needs, you know?"

"Yeah, right." Corliss pursed her lips. "You know you're not giving up the goodies until he makes you his wifey." She smiled affectionately. Her cousin was celibate, still at the age of twenty-five.

Back when she decided to move to Charlotte after studying Landscape Design at Art Institute, Caitlin was at Queens University and, of course, when she and Tanner met for the first time, her cousin was just a ponytail and braces wearing cutie with a huge crush. But, if she knew her cousin and, she certainly did, she would show twenty-nine-year-old Tanner what her intentions were, now that she would be commuting back and forth to Charlotte from the suburbs of Atlanta. Gavin was also twenty-nine and Corliss hoped he still held his bachelor's card. At twenty-eight, Corliss had mapped out a plan to be married with at least one child and working on two more by the age of thirty and knew that was her future with Gavin but, then, that night. *I've got it bad, still.*

Corliss recovered before her inquisitive cousin called her out for daydreaming of Gavin once again. "Look who is talking," Caitlin countered. "You might have not been a nun back in the day, but you sure put a stop to Gavin dipping in the cookie jar after, what? Two of those years?" Corliss felt her cheeks heat.

"Hush, that." She glanced around the crowded restaurant to see if anyone had heard her loud mouth cousin. But, indeed, Corliss had made up her mind; she wanted to harness the sexual side of their relationship until their impending nuptials, in which she knew would be their future. But it wasn't an easy promise to keep, especially when she and Gavin, who agreed to the vow, had to take plenty of ice-cold showers, letting them know they needed a little more restraint in that area. Corliss could only shake her head because the test hadn't even begun to measure how she felt then and even now. She wanted to whisk away all articles of clothing and have her way from sunrise to sunset with this man.

***

"So, she's back, so what?" Gavin whispered, shrugging broad shoulders in mock nonchalance. Tanner had long gone, leaving him to sulk in the news of Corliss being forced back into his life, but who was he kidding? It was a deal a very big deal. One that was causing the hammering *of* his *heart* to capitulate and brain befuddle in a puddle of mulch. With just the mere mention of her name, he was rattled and didn't like how she managed to have that much powering control over his senses. In learning she was back in Charlotte, he couldn't concentrate on his clients' master-bedroom retreat. Why did she still own his heart and thoughts when, obviously, she didn't want it nor deserve it, for that matter?

Setting his designer's graphic board aside and twirling its pencil between nimble fingers, Gavin continued his path down memory lane. The year was two-thousand and nine when he first laid eyes on the gorgeous and promising landscape design major.

She was the most intriguing young lady he had met since walking the campus of Art Institute of Atlanta. Not only was she pleasing on the outside, with supple latte mahogany-brown skin, exotic specks of golden hazel brown eyes, and a smile that was both endearing and sexy, she was smart and compassionate, and he was drawn to her like a bee to a honeycomb. Corliss had captured his heart, then crushed it like a power drill, wreaking its due diligence seven years later.

He needed to just relax and ride with the flow. Work with Corliss for a season or chance being canceled; he had to trust Tanner knew what he was doing, suggesting his old flame. She wasn't the only image consultant out there but, like he and his best friend knew, she specialized in working with design stars and was the producer of her own landscape blog and podcast; she was proven to be the best. And, right now, he knew what else he needed, and that was a visit to his ex-girlfriend, Veronica Edward's, home. The voluptuous former airline stewardess was sure to keep him preoccupied. Gavin made a mental note to call her first thing tomorrow to see if she was up for one of his visits. In one visit, he would be able to at least relieve a smidgen of the painful tension Corliss left him with when she walked out on him that night.

Second thought, Gavin stole a cursory glance at his Burberry wristwatch that read 9:15. Grabbing his cellphone, he decided to make the call. The woman's touch he grown to crave would be the kind of therapy he needed tonight, if he had it his way.

"Yeah. Right there, babe. Your hands are phenomenal," Gavin praised.

Veronica grinned and continued to knead the pressure points in Gavin's muscular back and broad shoulders. She allowed her hands to spray over the corded muscles appreciatively. Minutes later, she frowned slightly. "G, you are so tense. Who is she?" This made Gavin's eyes snap wide open.

"What did you say?"

Veronica chuckled, continuing to pleasure her ex. She owned Savvy Massage, a spa mobile service. "You heard me loud and clear, even if your girl, Sade's greatest hits, are playing in the background."

Gavin shrugged lightly. "I can't help it if I'm old school and happen to be star-struck by the gorgeous and tantalizing R&B artist. You know I met her once; I did tell you that, right? It was-"

Veronica laughed, causing Gavin to relish in the smokiness of her laughter over the sexy ballad. They dated off and on and were now just friends, but that didn't mean he couldn't still list off all of her fine attributes and the woman had plenty. Like now, her raspy and sexy voice alone would make any red-blooded male want to hear it in their ears when…

"Stop trying to avoid the question!" she chided, breaking into his thoughts over Sade's popular hit, *Sweetest Taboo*. "Who is she? Or I'll be forced to take these same hands and-"

"Okay. I hear you."

Veronica's hands went still. "Corliss," they said in chorus.

Gavin blew out a heavy sigh and started at the beginning. "Wow," Veronica murmured, once he finished recapping from why Corliss would be forced back into his universe. Ending with bated breath, Gavin paused for his ex-girlfriend to put her opinion on the table—nothing.

"Is that all?" he interjected, flipping fluidly on his back. He needed to see her facial expression to his question.

Veronica nonchalantly shrugged her shoulders. "Gav, you know as well as I do that you two have a history and it has never gotten resolved. So-"

"So? What are you saying V?" He was getting annoyed by the second. "So, you saying I should just let by-gones be by-gones? Now that she has rolled back in town? Cause I sure ain't feeling this return! Is that what you're saying? I'm supposed to be like 'let's pick up where I thought we had that 'real connection' kind of love before that night'?"

Veronica's eyes softened. Her heart went out to him. "Gavin, you still love her, you always have. Take it from me; if you will just swallow your pride and stop letting that big head of yours swell," she playfully swatted at his chiseled chest," you will know that she still lives in your heart and soul, so don't mess it up but work hard to repair the damage, okay? Now, turn back over before I forget we are friends!" she said.

Gavin grinned. "You're my girl, always gotta a brotha's back," he complied obediently or else. Gavin knew Veronica Edwards was dainty as they came, but had a 'kick-butt' persona. To say she was a tomboy would be a correct assessment. She would challenge him into a headache. The woman was a fierce competitor.

"Yeah, yeah, already." She returned a grin of her own. "Got me up doing you a service after ten at night. Shut up and I'm charging you double for the advice, too!"

Gavin chuckled. "That's my V for you. The lucky man in your life should know he has a keeper."

I thought it was you… but your heart belongs to her…
"Whatever man! My advice is not cheap and better not be wasted!"

Gavin heaved out a long breath. "I hear ya, V. I hear ya." Gavin left Veronica's with pep in his step. He felt refreshed and knew he would be sleeping like a baby once he hit his designer's sheets. Breathing in the cool brisk air of early May, Gavin allowed his body to soak in the invigorated service of his girl, Veronica. He always enjoyed being surrounded by nature's gift, although it had become a painful reminder in his childhood. He smiled serenely, still in effect mode of his massage. She had hands of a Goddess and had given him the 'in your face' advice he knew she would never hold back.

He and Veronica were always upfront with one another and that's what made their relationship so easily able to transition from lovers to friends, but sorry; he wasn't going to follow her sage advice, this time.

He thought Corliss would one day become his wife, but it didn't happen. If only he could let go of his stubborn streak and just maybe hear her out in the reason why she made the decision to walk out his life, but things happened for a reason and, obviously, her rolling back in town was for business only and needed to be left there. But, he was taking it personal and he didn't feel like being the bigger person.

Gavin smirked; his lips upturned in a guileful grin. He would seduce her, then turn around and give her a dose of her own medicine. Was it right? No, but what did they say about pay back? Yeah that…

Well dear heart, get ready to feel the wrath of yours truly. First, my father the austere reverend and then you—the one I trusted to be there for me…

       ***

Fifteen-minutes later, Gavin whipped his Mercedes Benz Coupe into his driveway in South Charlotte. He sat there a lingering moment, scheming out the details of how he would exact revenge. Of course, he knew it wasn't right, but he was sick and tired of feeling caged like an animal with bottled-up anger toward them both. He just wanted things to subside, especially because he still respected his father. Although their relationship had been strained over the years and since then, all over again when he overheard his father and coworker of the network talking what appeared to be an intimate conversation. Deep down, he knew he needed to forgive but, for Corliss, she wasn't family and he didn't expect to ever have to deal with her again. He could hold a grudge from afar, but the anger was gnawing him inside; he had to grudgingly admit to himself. And, where his mother was concerned, she was not privy of what really happened between Corliss and him and, certainly, she didn't know about his father's infidelity years ago that had started back, but she kept telling him to "let go and let God." He only further kept both betrayals inside, only sharing both with his boy, Tanner, who tried to get him to open up and approach his father about his cheating ways.

As for Corliss, he encouraged him to do the same. Gavin thought about his devious plan en route to his home. He was going to make her pay dearly for crushing his heart, as a sly grin crested his handsome face; he now had the perfect demise. She should have chosen to be there for him, no matter what.

"No, he didn't. The nerve of that man!" Corliss retorted aloud, flouncing herself back into her Honda Accord. Once all the details had been finally ironed out and she and Gavin's first matter of business a week later was to meet up for their first exercise, he had the nerve to cancel on her at the last second. Thank God she had told him to meet her at her office an hour before the actual time of their appointment. *Two can play that game...* Corliss knew that this was one of Gavin's ploys. She detected it in his voice.

Chapter Two

She knew him all too well and he was trying to rattle her; she smelled a snake. But, he would still have to work with her, whether the irresistible, pig-headed man wanted to play childish games along the way. Corliss shook her head in defiance. *No. I can't let you do this... I won't let you do this...*

Corliss knew there were deep issues surrounding Gavin's mood swings. She still knew him well and as Tanner had shared with her, an intervention was a dire must!

Corliss would work her business to the fullest and just as professional, keeping it in that zone, but for how long would she be able to keep her personal feelings, her love for him, at bay that was the winning question. Corliss started the engine and coasted toward interstate 1-77 north to Gavin's studio, A Designer's Muse, in Birkdale Village, Huntersville. She thought about how Gavin's stubbornness could really put a dagger in his career. She would not let that happen on her watch. Once she reached her destination and sought out the culprit, she was determined hard-ball was how she had to handle him for now on.

***

"Send me…" Gavin's words hung in the balance; he lifted his gaze from the conversation, colliding with a pair of angry, most beautiful, golden-brown eyes, pinning him disapprovingly. *The woman is even more beautiful angry; I've got to do something about this insane attraction towards her,* he thought. Gavin gulped. He knew he was in a world of trouble. Hurricane Corliss had entered the building. Well, let the 'cat and mouse' games begin. He was ready for round two. "Excuse me, Crystal." Gavin threw a quick acknowledgement over his shoulder to Crystal Lewis, his design assistant. Gavin was thankful she was on his creative design team; she was truly an asset and, after interning last year, he confidently hired her on four months ago when his former assistant, Hannah, decided to become a stay home mom.

"No problem, boss." Crystal grinned flirtatiously. Corliss thought she saw a glitter of interest beyond professional in Crystal's blue eyes. The young twenty something was batting her lashes so hard; Corliss couldn't help to notice they were gorgeously long; she was gorgeous, for that matter. Was he dating her? *No… Gavin was a complete professional; he would not cross that code of ethic…*

Corliss's heart sank at the very thought of competing with the beach-babe blonde. Fresh, painful memories of Gavin cheating on her four years ago flooded Corliss' mind. She wanted to turn on her heels and leave him standing there once again. But, she had a job to do, and anything personal past or present had to be erased from her schema.

Before she knew it, Gavin was standing directly in front of her; his hot gaze roved lazily over the length of her body, searing her skin in an inferno she hoped didn't show. But, judging by the perspiration that now dotted her skin, she knew that he had. Corliss feathered her right hand at the base of her neck and nervously cleared her throat. He always knew how to obliterate her concentration with a smoldering gaze, just as he was purposefully doing now.

"Don't try to distract me, don't do it Gavin." She shook her head slowly, when what she really wanted to do was lift up on her toes and kiss that knowing smirk off his full lips. Gavin gestured her down the winding hallway and into his office, closing the door before he turned around wistfully and regarded her.

"If you can't take the heat, baby, then I suggest you concede while you can." He winked as he strolled lazily behind his desk and began leafing through its content with meticulous scrutiny.

Was he dismissing her? Oh, snap! Corliss made her way further into his office, slapping a hand on her hip. "What's a little heat between ex-lovers?" She skewered him a deadpan look. Gavin's face scrunched up and she could tell he didn't like the flippant comeback. But, she didn't care. He was going to take this intervention like a man. A grown man!

"Please," Gavin chuckled softly. "That was water under an old bridge. I'm about new and innovative, sweetheart, just like my career."

"Was, Gavin," she gently countered. "Your media career is in the 'red', so, 'get your life'," Corliss quipped in the popular catchphrase of Tamar Braxton from the R&B family's reality show, Braxton's Family Values.

"Oh, so when did you become a fan of reality shows?" He laughed, with mirth behind his words; Corliss knew. Gavin was a man who didn't show much humor when it came at his dispense, so he was trying to compensate to throw her off. She knew he was struggling to remain in control.

"You stand to learn some pointers from the ones that are still making the ratings," she threw back at him. *Low blow, but she was pulling out all of her weapons.*

"Say what?" Gavin frowned. She sauntered over to Gavin, placing her palms across the Executive chrome desk.

"You ready to play nicely?" She smirked.

"It depends," he smoothly supplied.

Corliss sucked in a frustrated breath and blew out a heavy gust of air. This man was thinning her patience like a sheer of silk. *Two months can't come fast enough,* she thought. "Okay, I'll bite. It depends on what? I dare ask?" Gavin leaned in close to her ear while delicately stroking the back of his hand along the path of her jaw, searing her skin in a white hot desire that she wanted to give into but knew she dare not go down that road again.

"Have dinner with me tonight, love."

Corliss could only manage a quick shake of her head, no. Her stomach quivered in a swirl of butterflies. A hot and faint feeling up surged in her gut and her voice lodged thickly in her throat, as she inwardly took in the comfort of his sensual touch. Turning away, she blinked back the tears she knew would be plentiful, clouding her vision if she didn't get the heck out of there and fast. "Gavin," she blew out a ragged breath, extricating his hand from her face. She needed to draw her distance from his burning touch. Stepping back, Corliss instantly missed the warmth of his minty breath that fanned her right cheek like a dulcet breeze of fresh air. It had taken her to a place of respite but, then, she remembered where her mission lied and it wasn't to become caught up in the magnetism of Gavin Nathaniel McCoy. Hadn't she been stung enough to know why she couldn't go there with him, again?

"Yes?" He perked up.

"Gather your things for your first exercise, remember?" Corliss flipped her auburn shoulder-length tresses to one side with a shaky finger, beckoning him to follow as she strolled out of his office on wobbly legs while managing to put one foot in front of the other. Once Corliss secured his door and closed it, her hand paused around the brushed nickel door knob; she caught her breath that she didn't realize she was holding. With a confident grin, she whispered, "Nice try, though."

As Corliss made her way toward the swanky, jazz-inspired reception, she heard laughter above the soft jazz floating through hidden speakers. The two designers comprised of Gavin's junior designers were milling around the art-deco modern lounge adjacent, and she decided to stop in for a quick chat. "Hi," Dana Miller greeted with a bright smile.

Reese Stewart grinned. "Well, hello there."

"Good morning." Corliss returned a friendly grin. She liked them instantly, after being introduced two weeks ago. Both were creative and talented designers with bubbly personalities, and Gavin was blessed to have snagged the duo. Both had their own eclectic style and aligned well with what style Gavin was marketing: fresh, innovative, and modern with a blend of art deco. She was so proud of Gavin accomplishing his dream as founder and CEO of his own firm and celebrity stardom, but he had a lot more work to do to maintain his media presence, and that's where she came in, not in the personal life of a man she knew she would always love but couldn't have the 'happily ever-after'.

"Boss man decided he better make it after all, huh?" Dana asked as she offered Corliss a platter of assorted pastries. "Try one, they are yummy!"

"Why thank you," Corliss said, choosing a lemon crusty one. After taking a dainty bite, she moaned. "Hmmm, these are delicious," she uttered around a bite full. She didn't want to be the rumor around the studio but, since obviously Gavin must've shared their field trip planned today, she shrugged. "He is not getting rid of me any time soon." Corliss winked and held her hand up for a high-five, "To girl power!"

"To girl power!" Dana mimicked, slapping a high five with Corliss. The two erupted in a spill of giggles. Reese shook his head, suppressing a grin.

"You ladies are brutal. Remind me not to ever get on either of your bad side."

"Why, Reese?" Dana gave him a sweet, innocent doe-look with a bat of her thick, long lashes. "We are perfectly innocent."

Reese softly chuckled. "Right... okay, whatever you say."

"Whatever," Dana clucked her tongue and playfully rolled her eyes at him. She turned her attention back to Corliss. "Care for something to drink?" she asked while waving her hand in the direction of the full-sized stainless steel refrigerator. "We have apple, orange, cranberry juice, bottled water and, of course," she eyed the top of the line Ninja coffee maker, "all assortment of coffee, blends. I can hook you up with some hazelnut if you like?"

Corliss narrowed her gaze playfully. "How did you know hazelnut was my favorite? But, no thank you. I actually need to get to the exercise site. I'll take a bottled water to go though, please. Thanks," she accepted, reaching for the chilled Deer Park Reese had quickly supplied.

"Perhaps a little birdie might have shared that little info." Dana winked in a wide grin.

"Hmm. I see, a little birdie, huh?"

"Okay, I hear you. I'm headed that way now," Gavin retorted and blew out a deep breath. His jaw ticked in frustration as he listened to Tanner rattled off how he had received a text message from Corliss stating she was on her way to drag him to his ice-breaker exercise, and that he knew the situation would be well taken care of, knowing the persistent Corliss. "Well… yeah, she was rather pushy. But, let me holla at you later…" his sentence faltered, as he drove up to the location in wonderment of, again, why she wanted him to meet her here.

Gavin remembered earth-tone lips pursed into the cutest bow when she simply told him to be ready to get his hands dirty. So, without preamble, since she showed up at the studio after he cancelled on her, he decided to change into a pair of blue Boot cut denim jeans and yellow American Eagle t-shirt he absently packed that morning. He met smirking grins and frowned at his staff as he passed them in the atrium.

"What you starring at?" he asked them. "Get back to designing!" He didn't need them making fun. *Who does she think she is, summoning me anywhere? Now my staff think I'm a wimp!*

"Gavin?"

Gavin blinked rapidly, realizing Tanner was still on the line. "I-I can't believe she went there-"

"Gavin. Don't mess things up, you here?" Tanner warned.

"Whatever, dude. Bye."

Gavin maneuvered into a parking space further from the building he was expected to enter and tried measuring the breaths that came in spurts. Was he having an anxiety attack or worse, a heart-attack?

The memories Gavin didn't want to re-visit were now front and center of his brain. "Just great!"

"What is all of this?" Gavin frowned slightly as he gazed over the supplies of hoes, shovels, and wheelbarrows. He turned fully toward the rest of the space where Corliss had set up stake.

"I remember when you said one of your biggest inspirations was to create a cool outside learning environment for children. So, here is your opportunity to do so!"

Gavin heard the excitement in her voice. The corners of his mouth twitched annoyingly.

"Are you serious right now?" Memories of that day corralled his brain. But, what did that conversation have to do with reviving his media presence? He didn't sign up for childish games on the grounds of a schoolyard. His former one had pretty much left a bad taste in his mouth, since that dreadful day he witnessed his father embracing his mistress a little too intimately.

He was nine-years-old and, even during that innocent stage of his life, he knew the hug couldn't have been an innocent one. He remembered backing away and scurrying off to anywhere as fast as his bony legs would allow him. How could his father disrespect his mother like that? Gavin still couldn't wrap his brain around it. His mother was not only beautiful outside but inside as well, as the most compassionate and giving individual he knew. And especially, right up under her nose, his father didn't deserve her not one bit. But, Gavin knew that his mother also had a vulnerable side; he wished she would grow a backbone when it came to his father. She always ended up taking a backseat to his aspirations and goals.

His mother taught second grade at the school and to know they were obviously parading their disgust of a romance with no regards of her catching them in their actions was just as pathetic. The very thought of his mother discovering in that way turned his stomach.

When he shared his inspirations with Corliss that day, they were a fountain of wet behind the ears youths, still at the ages eighteen and nineteen. He shared that little tidbit while they were on the subject of landscape design at the university's student café. They had recently started dating; she was a landscape major and he was in the second year of his interior design major. But, what Corliss didn't know was that was a childhood pipe dream he was sharing, a painful one at that, long before witnessing his father, the physical education teacher, and botanical teacher, embracing that day after-school. But, he remembered their conversation like it was yesterday; she looked adorable, her personality infectious, and her inspiration—passionate in someday designing a natural environment where children could have two of both worlds, a creative physical space and green environment to promote learning and a healthier, overall lifestyle.

Corliss, the woman who captured his heart and soul back then and, to this day, she still imprisoned it; he didn't have the heart to duce her exuberance and he didn't feel like being there in the first place. Gavin shook his head and gruffly protested.

"I didn't sign up for this, Cor."

"Well… actually you did," she informed him, "when you signed on the dotted line."

Gavin was stunned speechless. A brutal punch knocked at his gut. He couldn't break down in front of her. *Pull it together man; don't let her see you sweat. Keep composed at all cost.*

Chapter Three

Brilliant blue skies and a valley of vibrant and bountiful trees surrounded a beautiful spring day, capturing nature's miraculous beauty on canvas. And, as the wind stirred a gentle breeze, the sun kissed a warm caress over her dewy skin. Corliss felt sure this day was the perfect backdrop to getting Gavin on board of rekindling his love for nature. She guessed it was a not so and either the setting was dead wrong, or the whole idea was a ground zero. Judging by Gavin's body language, she was nowhere near in the vicinity of scoring the winning homerun.

"Come on." She tugged lightly at his muscular arm. He was wearing the v-cut t-shirt like a second layer of skin; she openly admired his arms of steel, chiseled chest, and washboard pectorals. He was built like a Greek God!

Good Lord! She mumbled and sighed. A pair of denim jeans hugged at his muscular, slightly bowed legs, and those toned thighs… a zap of raw awareness curled up Corliss' spine, causing the release of a soft moan to escape her lips. And that was not all, for the life of her, she couldn't peel an eyeful away. Seconds later while clearing her throat, she added, "Let's get you checked-in to the office, so we can get started; the students should be arriving to the worksite shortly." She graced him with a bright smile.

Here she was drooling over this man like she did when she first met on the campus of AI. *Get a grip… remember?* Well, she was also human and she was tempted to say the heck with the past.

"It's for the kids, remember?" She chided when she heard him smack kissable lips.

"Hmm," he replied.

"Come on now. Cheer up!"

"I am all about cheering up," he told her. "Since the chance to get my hands dirty with you, again."

"Don't you dare!" she shielded her face, turning her back to him.

"Too late," he laughed with mischief while reaching down to grab a patch of dirt, then throwing it at her.

"Stop it, you! Be the adult here!" She giggled, darting back and forth. The dirt landed squarely at her backside.

"Bingo!" He winked.

Corliss grinned and shook her head. This man… this man… what am I going to do with him? Let him into your heart again, a small voice echoed in her conscience.

Again? Corliss knew he hadn't ever left her heart; he still owned it and even more now. If she would only face the fact of the matter.

Gavin let out a low whistle, pleasuring her with a cocky grin when Corliss glanced over her shoulder, giving him a saucy grin. "You better act like you've been home trained, young man."

We could easily get back in the routine of jarring with one another, Gavin thought to himself, but he had to play the role like an academy A-list actor and not succumb to her. "Eh. You let me decide whether I want to put those 'home training' skills," he gestured with his fingers "to good use, here. All is fair in basketball or…" he looked around at his surroundings, "by the nature trail."

"You are stupid!" Corliss teased, erupting in a carefree laugh. She could easily get back in the routine of just enjoying a stress-free, fun time with Gavin. If only she could tear down that brick wall he built to protect himself. Was it because of her? Was he trying to protect himself from her? How could that be when he was the one who cheated and tried to act kosher, like it was nothing but a chicken wing the very night she was going to expose him for it?

Corliss' brain raced like a meet at the Kentucky Derby. She was anxious of the possibility of their second-chance. They entered into the hall of Martin Academy elementary toward the school administrative office and Corliss had made up her mind. She would not let Gavin get her all giddy again. She had one goal and one goal in mind. Do her job. Coach him up. Save his media image and syndication, then out of his life she would ride off into the sunset.

All leading to one mission accomplished. Period. After checking-in and meeting the office staff, Gavin and Corliss made the return to the work site. Gavin stared in amazement. Corliss was in her element. Gavin observed the fiery passion in her eyes, as she quickened her strolls towards the field to greet a group of excited students. Landscaping was not only her profession, but he remembered her mentioning that, one day when she had children herself, she wanted to pass along the appreciation of nature with them. And, today, you could tell as she laid out her plan with the children to begin a landscaping project that had her immensely invested.

Observing the students' faces, they were sold in creating the magical nature trail she had envisioned for the space. She was pretty darn spectacular, he had to admit. He wasn't at all surprised how successful she had become with her own PR firm, Prime Image, Incorporated, that was going to coach him up in enhancing his media image and he knew she, of all people, could make it happen. She was definitely his superwoman and she made it look flawless. But had he placed her on a pedestal, thinking she could handle everything perfectly and with effortless precision? Had he been unfair to her all of this time?

Gavin wanted her still something fierce, galvanizing him in a way no other woman had ever been able to do since. But, he couldn't put his heart out there for her to do even more damage. He couldn't chance it with her while so many conflicting variables presented a surmounting load of distractions. His father showing out again resulting in him keeping more secrets from his naïve mother; his father being called into the ministry and retiring to accept an associate minister position at New Generations Ministries six years ago, with access to more women vying for his attention, didn't help the situation.

Theodore Clyde McCoy was a natural born philander. He'd observed him over the years and he had a way with the ladies. And, then, his mother also retiring and heeding to her calling into the ministry and as a housewife, again after only teaching ten years, she stayed in the shadows of his father. And Gavin didn't like it. But, she was very instrumental in the ministry and had a niche for outreach and had orchestrated many of the church's community and church events over the years. Gavin wondered if maybe his mother needed to become more in tuned with her husband's outgoing personality and how it obviously impacted his faithfulness to his wife over the years.

And all of the drama spilling over in his media career that he had to admit was wreaking havoc when it came to his personal life these days.

Corliss teetered between anticipation and hesitancy as the crew worked busily side-by-side on preparing the ground work for the extension of a nature trail experience. Gavin had told her he already could envision what he wanted to design for the space. She knew it would be amazing. He was so talented and she was happy he already felt just as passionate.

She chanced this form of therapy would be good for him and, so far, it had. The students were chatter boxes and Gavin was awesome engaging in their slew of questions. He answered their questions with much fervor and patience. She knew he loved children and told her plenty of times during the course of their relationship that he wanted at least four little McCoy's frolicking around in their home someday. Was that even their future? Could they still have their love and their family?

Gavin assisted with the wheelbarrow and trudging the mound of dirt, and Corliss knew he was photographing a mental picture of every detail of space management and design.

A dark cloud shadowed Gavin's features for a millisecond, noticeably enough time for Corliss to know it was more than a 'thought mode' moment. She wondered what happened in his life recently that was causing him heartache?

"Are you okay, McPherson?" she leaned into him and asked above a whisper. The students were in their own little world. The elated conversations the students were having got her feeling adventurous in more ways than one.

"Uh. Yeah, why?"

She could tell he was caught off guard by her insight. Corliss briskly shrugged her shoulders as she went back to working on the ground work. "No reason, I guess," she murmured.

"Look. I'm fine. No worries. Although, I gotta admit. This is therapeutic."

Her brows shot up. "Really?"

"Really." He pleasured her with a handsome grin. "You did good, girl. I- I needed this. And let me try again... you gotta let me take you to dinner. How's tonight?"

Corliss adamantly shook her head. "Nope. Not tonight. I have a landscaping speaking engagement early tomorrow morning. Besides, I'm sure your social calendar on a Friday night is filled to capacity. A date or two..."

She was fishing and, by the sidelong glance he was giving her, she knew he knew the deal.

"Trying to find out if I'm single, Miss Adams?" He quirked an eyebrow.

"Really?" she choked out. "Please. I could care less-,"

"Ms. Adams! Look who's here!" A small statured, red-haired girl turned her attention towards Corliss. And she was thankful for the intrusion. She didn't need Gavin psychoanalyzing her intention.

Gavin lifted his gaze at the woman who trekked towards them wearing a gallant of a grin on her white, porcelain face. He remembered that face anywhere. His heart galloped in his chest. Is this some kind of cruel joke? Gavin hurled through gritted teeth.

"Nana!"

The older woman beamed; walking swiftly to meet up with the young girl with outstretched arms, she enveloped her tightly. "Oh... my dearest Aniline!" she cried.

Gavin slowly stood erect and inclined his head towards the direction of the older woman and young girl. Apparently, they were family. Gavin now saw the close resemblance. He watched the interaction with heated intensity. Was this planned? And did Corliss know about this? Gavin's mind raced and thoughts of the past plummeted like a rocket ship ready to blast off into the painful cosmos of his childhood memories. It came soaring back; just the mere thought squeezed his chest in a tight ball of tension.

"What's wrong?" Corliss' eyebrows knitted in confusion.

Gavin snapped his dark eyes at her. "You tell me Corliss?" he demanded in a hushed tone. "Did you know she would be here?" Fixing an index finger in the direction of the lady who in tow with the young girl, draped around her tiny waist. Both wearing wide grins, Gavin wanted to wipe the jovial expressions off their faces.

"Did you know that she is the culprit of my father's infidelity? Did. You. Know. This!"

Chapter Four

Corliss' chest tightened and she bristled inwardly under Gavin's terse tone. He was furious and she had no clue as to why he was angry with her. She felt her heart stall in her chest, becoming brewed with anger herself.

"Excuse me? Don't you dare use that tone with me! And what on earth are you talking about?" She was beyond floored with what he was implying that she had a sinister plan, or something to cause him to become infuriated. *"Yes! You hurt me beyond words could ever express, but I wouldn't stoop to intentionally hurting you… I still love you, you knucklehead!"* Corliss wanted to add; instead, she bit back her snide remarks, suppressing the urge of going crazy woman off on his pompous behind.

Gavin tossed her a wry smile. "Right. So, you're saying you had no idea Ms. Wren, the botanical teacher, would be gracing us with her lovely presence," he said with disdain.

He watched how she bristled at the way he was coming after her. He surprised even himself in the venomous way he addressed the woman after his own heart. His mother would take him down a notch or two if she'd heard how he'd spoken to her.

"Look, Miss Adams! My nana was able to make it after all!"

Chapter Five

Gavin pinned Corliss a dark scowl. "Yeah, Miss Adams, look who the wind blew in?" he husked. *Calm yourself down, bro! You're letting your emotions boil you over into a hot mess that's about to combust.*

Gavin could feel he was going to blow a gasket. He wanted to say more, but this was not the appropriate place. Instead, he sighed deeply, an unreadable expression flashed on his face. "Excuse me everyone," he turned and acknowledged the students still engrossed in the planting activity, along with their teachers. He was glad they seemed oblivious of what was going on, but he knew they all could sense the tension emitting from his reaction to Aniline's grandmother.

Corliss spoke up quickly. Clearing her voice audibly, she replied, "That's fine, honey." Turning to face their guest, she smiled, softly. "Hello Mrs. Olmstead," Corliss respectfully greeted with a shake of her hand. "I'm so glad you could make it. I apologize, but I do need to excuse myself," she said with a broad smile, "but, please do carry on students. I shall return."

She and Gavin strolled out of earshot of the group and made their way down the winding path where the Enchanting Garden would be created. After the coast was clear, she turned to him quietly. She was going to let him flat have it! Acting like a whiny two-year old. Where was the temper tantrum? He needed to be brought down a peg or two, for sure! Oh, she was ready to do the honors.

"I believe you owe me and everyone an apology back there." She furrowed her eyebrows and waved her hand horizontally toward the throngs of students and teachers.

Corliss now understood why he was so closed off, but he had to take control of his emotions, still. Saltiness was not a good flavor on him. She sympathized with the uncomfortable situation when obviously the now, Mrs. Olmstead, and his father had an affair, but she couldn't understand why he was so angry with her? Corliss had only met Mrs. Olmstead twice, so what gives with all the hostility?

Corliss furrowed a brow. No. She was not going to be Gavin's verbal punching bag! The inflicting pain was not her fault and she wasn't going to take ownership. *"Deal with it Gavin,"* she whispered under her breath. She was about to say those exact words louder and to his freaking face, but she froze because the man standing across from her had a way of rendering her speechless or muted, as her words dare not reach his ears, unless he acted as though they were not worth hearing.

Gavin's mouth was agape. He noted the chastising expression she was giving him. After all that she had put him through, he still didn't want to experience the backlash of her disapproval. So, he clamped his lips shut. The chiming of his cell interrupted the rant he was preparing to unleash on the woman he couldn't deny he still had strong feelings for.

Feeling for the device clipped to his denim waist, he shot a glance at the caller ID before swiping at the green lit up 'answer' tab. It was his mother and Gavin immediately became alarmed. Yes. He heard her bite off what he knew was something challenging but, whatever it was, he was going to ignore because when he wanted her to tell him that night why she was breaking up with him.

Corliss cocked her head to the side and glared at him in that 'sista girl' sardonic smirk. And the look he was getting from her now was just as icy.

Gavin knew, that night, Corliss' body language was meant to convey that he was given her that bunch of you-know-what-crap. Well, too bad… in his book, she didn't get to speak her mind now. Too late for the soap opera version! Her excuses meant absolutely nothing to him. Of course, his traitor of a heart spoke another love language, though. Maybe, in a matter of time, once he fulfilled this contract and got his stuff together in his head, he could move on and that meant move on from her without a head-turn in her vicinity. Yep. That was the game plan now, if he only believed it was that easy to walk away from her. She was not going to leave him strapping up his fraternity's signature gold boots; like it was yesterday, he remembered when she dropped the bomb that night. He had just finished up with a step show on the yard and was now confronted with the sordid news. Gavin wanted to fall on his knees and cry like he'd just got his butt tore up from the floor up from his father's heavy-laden hand.

"I have to take this," he murmured, warranting a quick glance in Corliss' direction.

He couldn't make direct eye contact? Corliss thought, which made her even angrier. *So, it was like that, now?* He couldn't stand to look at her?

Distancing himself from her to take the call, Gavin heard his mother and what sounded like a faint sniffing, as soon as he covered his ear to the device. His heart rate lurched into hyper drive. Gavin blew out lingered breaths. Something was not right.

"Mom? What's wrong?" he asked breathless. Was she crying? A mixture of anger and concern coated Gavin's expression. And was it his father's doing? It better not be... Gavin could feel his anger rising at uncharted height. And he was about to ramble off some choice words but stopped himself before doing so. His father better not be the reason why his mother had been crying. He hated to see his mother shed tears and wasted on a man who obviously didn't give a flip and wasn't worth the moisture flooding her pupils. Assuming his mother was probably in a state of despair, Gavin wanted to come through the phone and anchor, shutdown whatever it was causing Gretchen McCoy all the distress.

"Gavin," his mother's calm, velvety tone preened him out of his reverie, "settle down baby. I'm all right. But can you come by the house?"

"I'm on my way. Sorry." He tapped at his phone to end the conversation. His gaze collided with hers and held. Gavin, for the life of him, felt compelled to a stare down. And why not? The woman was breathtakingly gorgeous. Holding Corliss' gaze longer than he cared, Gavin sensed she felt the same. At least he knew that it wouldn't be hard to get her to fall for him like she had before. And what about himself? Okay. He'd admit he wasn't over, not even a twinge, but he couldn't let on and give her any indication he was going to let her off the hook. He had to keep on the façade mask.

After almost four years ago, so much had happened since then, professionally and personally, but the way Gavin saw it, all roads intersected back to painful highways and byways and he had hoped, no prayed, that he had a girlfriend that would be by his side and not running in the opposite direction.

There he was pouring out his soul, sweat, and tears after all that had transpired; she might as well have slapped him figuratively on his face. Gavin still felt the sting of her betrayal like it was yesterday:

"Gavin, it's over. Do not try to contact me because what we had isn't worth saving."

Gavin shook his head woefully as he tried to comprehend what the love of his life, his better half, was dishing off. She couldn't believe they were over. He wasn't going to sign-off on that. He was going to fight for their love, their future.

"I'm not losing you…" he murmured. His heart felt like a boulder of rocks had crashed his ribcage. "Tell me why this is happening, to us?" Gavin remember pleading…

And although they say time healed a broken heart, Gavin knew time stood still and continued to rip his heart out in agony; like an amputation of a limb, he felt the dismembered just as deep, just as present.

Corliss nodded her understanding. The air cloaked in palpable tension. At least, he could now look at her minus the scowl. Sprinting in the direction of the parking lot, he yelled over his shoulder. "I've got to jet! We'll talk later," he pointedly confirmed, giving her the 'I'm not at all finish with this… not by a long shot', look.

And with a turn of his sculpted back, Gavin moved like a leopard with purposeful strides to his automobile, leaving Corliss in wonderment of what his mother urgently needed for him to dash out in such a hurry? She pressed her index finger lightly to her lips. If he kept this up, the behavior, fight vs. flight syndrome, was going to send his blood pressure soaring through the chimney roof. Corliss had a feeling all the mess he bottled inside was bound to combust and she had to do something, anything to disarm the repercussions. Operation-in-action was the mission and Corliss was determined to dismantle the lock before Gavin locked the safe to his embedded pain.

Corliss was seconds in tearing a penetrating gaze from burning a hole in Gavin's retreating back, when she stifled the words that nestled in her spirit, "Let me back into your world..." She felt a light palm of a small hand grasp her right shoulder. "I'm so sorry..."

Corliss worried her lips in a tremble. She wanted to breakdown in an outpour of how she felt, helpless, and glanced back to see that it was Mrs. Olmstead with a concern expression on her wrinkled face. She had to be in her late fifties from doing the math she had shared that she'd taught for twenty-nine years, but the woman before her looked as though she had been through the hard doggy-dog life, appearing twice her age.

"I must've upset the young man, no?"

Corliss paused in her rebuttal. It wasn't her place to get in the middle of Gavin's personal business. She was only here to renew his professional prowess and that was all, so why was she the suitor of his excessive baggage, and what baggage it all was, and she didn't need this kind of drama.

She found herself reaching out for the older woman's hands. "It's his battle, not yours."

Why was this lady acting as if she knew Gavin, personally? Did she? Had she remembered how she made a mess of things?

Chapter Six

Mrs. Olmstead replied gingerly, "No dear, you see, the battle is not his. Like Yolanda Adams says, it's the Lord's. So, young lady, be there for him and be in prayer for your friend. He has a lot of pent up emotions I gather."

Yeah. And you are the reason why...

Corliss smiled cordially and nodded. Who was she to judge anyone? And yet, that's what she was doing? *You don't know this woman's heart...* what a wise woman. She must have a deep testimony. "You're right," she acquiesced. "I will. And I'm praying he knows that as well."

What was she talking about? Of course he did. Gavin may be stubborn as a bull-headed mule, but he was a man of faith. When they were dating and she wanted to say 'the heck with it', whether it was an exam she was not sure if she would pass or one of her girlfriends tried to sway her in the opposite direction of her new life in Christ, Gavin was in her ear, encouraging her to speak over herself and encourage herself in the Lord. And so, she knew he knew a little something about having faith as small as a mustard seed. God. She missed him, the powerful connection they shared once was special, bonding. She couldn't shake that it wasn't there anymore. Or was it?

Corliss wanted to go after him. But, instead, she decided to give Gavin the much needed space. But, time was money and money was time. It came down to saving his media career and possibly more on that shelf. But, now based on what transpired here, Corliss' perspectives had a whole new view and she planned to peck away at the tender, sore surfaces of Gavin's pain. Helping him into forgiving himself first, in which she felt in her spirit, Gavin, was casting all the blame on his shoulders. But, why? That was what she planned on searching down deep to find the answer.

***

"Shut your mouth!"

Corliss could just imagine her cousin's ears perking, alert of a red-flag from the news she was sharing and, although over the phone, she could just imagine Caitlin perched at the end of her home office chair, ready to engage in some good old 'Stop it! Girl, you lying!' gossip.

This was his present demon keeping him to release the beast. And her cousin was taking the news lightly? Like, really? Corliss could admit; she could also entertain some hot gossip, but it wasn't Corliss' intention to get in some idle mess with her cousin; she wasn't sharing it for some channel nine news reporting. Rolling her eyes in dramatic form, Corliss' shook her head forcefully. "We are not having this conversation for personal entertainment. You know this is homework for us, right?"

A deep sigh resonated over the airwaves of Corliss' ear buds. "I know," Caitlin finally relented. "But, dang it. I sometimes like to engage in some harmless gossip chit chat every once in a while, like the next person. But, all right, go ahead and spill," she playfully laughed. "I'll behave, girl scout's honor!" Corliss could see her silly cousin reenacting the Scout's pledge. The girl was too much!

Corliss shook her head. "Be serious. This is Gav's livelihood." And why was she in Gavin's protective armor mode? Who cheated on whom?

"Girl… that man's wound up too tight if you ask me! So… what's the new game plan? Because I know you have one. I can imagine the wheels churning in that brain of yours."

Corliss exhaled in frustration. She felt a dull headache brewing. "We're going to have to break down those walls and, trust, I know it won't be easy." No. It won't be, but Corliss was going to put on her boxing gloves and duke it out with Gavin, so be it. Corliss knew even a tiny morsel that she wanted more than regaining his trust; she wanted answers. Corliss wanted closure of the relationship they once had, and the only way to get that was to understand what factors led to the dishonesty he chose to feed her that night they parted ways barely on speaking terms through the years. So, why in the heck did she take him on as a client when it could all blow up in her face?

Like her mother, Clara Reynolds Adams, always declared she had always been good at what she did for her clients. And, even better, Christian who reaches out to others, looking to build them up, instead of knocking them down to the knees. Sure, she was tough as nails and she got in her clients' faces, but she genuinely looked for the ups and as much as possible and downplayed the negatives. And that's what she planned on doing with Gavin. He had to let her in. "But with a little elbow grease, we can do it. And believe it's going to take a lot of that to do just that with him," she replied firmly.

Unlike her cousin, she had the patience of Job and she was going to have to exercise even more of it to hurdle this obstacle by the name of Gavin McCoy. "But, it's not impossible," she heard herself admit. Groaning, she pressed, "This could be a migraine waiting to happen. I hate to insert myself in a client's personal life like this but this calls for an exception because maybe the crest of why his professional life is in a fray of shambles has a lot to do with his father's betrayal."

"Sounds like you've got yourself a personal situation. I'm just saying. You know the 'in love' kind? No shade girl but, if you ask me," Caitlin snickered, "you know like the dope hit Usher croons about? You've Got It Bad, lady!"

"Whatever, diva! You're something else."

Caitlin slanted a side-eyed; although, her cousin couldn't see her expression. Her oval-shape face lit up like Times Square on New Year's Eve, dawning that she just had proof in the pudding that her straight-laced cousin and best friend was not all that over with their newest client. Trying to act like she was over the fine brotha.

"Whatever. You," she swirled her rose-petal red, manicured finger in the air, "are still in love with ole boy. So, tell me. What ya planning on doing about it, mama?"

Corliss blew out a winded breath, swiping a hand across her hairline. She strolled hastily to her car as she pondered on what the heck she was going to do about it, or the man that could be just as stubborn as she could. She had finished with briefing the students and, when the rest of the volunteers and a crew from Home Depot arrived, the show went on, but she couldn't help to worry about if Gavin's mother was okay. She'd met Mr. and Mrs. McCoy and liked them instantly. Mrs. McCoy was a sweetheart and always welcomed her. She could imagine she wasn't going to be accepted by his family and invited to anymore family reunions.

Corliss was not only physically exhausted, she was mentally, and needing to decompress was an understatement. She was going to treat herself to lunch and maybe waltz in on one of her favorite gourmet bakeries for a delicious dozen of Scarlet Red Velvet cupcakes. Enough of the racing thoughts! She shook her head in frustration and answered Caitlin, who she knew was like an 'inquiring minds' want to know reporter.

"That's the Jeopardy question of the day, my dear cousin. I haven't a clue…" Would she be able to get through this intact, professionally, and without falling even harder for this man? She was already in it deeper than she'd told herself she would allow.

Chapter Seven

Gavin veered into his parents' driveway in the affluent Huntersville subdivision and scanned his surroundings. His mother's silver BMW sedan was the only car in the driveway. Unless his father's matching but black BMW was parked in the two-car garage in which he normally kept it, along with his SUV, he wasn't at the residence.

Gavin's face contorted in anger. "You've got to be kidding me… he out on my mom?" he muttered. Gavin bit back a string of expletives that were at the tip of his tongue and stretched his long torso behind the steering wheel, while schooling his emotions not to overreact. His mother did say she was fine. So, he released a fortifying breath but, with legs feeling like lead in each step he made towards his parent's front door, Gavin couldn't help to journey in his childhood memories of how he felt when he saw his father embracing Ms. Wren. It was like déjà vu all over again seeing Barbara Wren, the woman whom yielded to a married man, and that man being his father in whom he looked up to was his hero, and no one could tell him his dad was not a saint.

And, now, the present situation with Vivian Armstrong, his colleague of the network. The beautiful and eloquent replica of a younger Nancy Wilson appeared to be fawning over his father. Whenever his dad would visit the network, she made sure she was there when she could to flirt, of course maintaining the professional but, never the less, outright flirtation it was. Gavin didn't want to disrespect his elder, so he held back his recoil. When he asked his father whether there was something going on, he shrugged and honestly admitted Vivian was a beautiful woman and it was nothing going on there, but he was flattered by her appreciation of him. That did not sit well with Gavin. Here he was in ministry leadership and he still kept that playa swagger.

Gavin did not get it. His deceitful ways not only hurt his only child but, more importantly, his wife and Gavin didn't want to but he did; deep down, he knew he had some deep-seated hatred for his father's past discretions and who said he was more than flattered by Vivian. For so long, knowing that he went around preaching even back then about honoring God and all about the commandments ingrained in Gavin's mind; it was like a flashing 'don't-go-there' neon sign of the commandment Thou shall not commit adultery! Remember that one?

"Gavin, your father went to the pharmacy. He should be back shortly. I wanted to talk to you before he returned. He wanted to be here, though," his mother shook her head firmly, "but I told him I needed this time with our only son first. I think perhaps, over the years, I led you to believe we weren't really happy, me and your father." She shrugged her shoulders. "Sure, everything wasn't always beautiful as a rose garden, but we love each other. Always have and I believe always will. And so…"

Gavin felt like the wind had been knocked out of his windpipe. He wished his mother would just come out with it because the suspense was making him stir crazy. He leaned forward and braced himself for what he knew was going to be displeasuring news.

"Mom... what are you saying? Are you ill?" He felt a pang in his stomach. The room had begun to tilt. "You-you said over the phone it was okay, but... and you had been crying…" What was his mother trying to tell him? Gavin braced himself, but he felt a tense muscle in his neck that had already started its ache-filled pain.

"Hon, it's not anything of that nature. I'm sorry I alarmed you. Your father is picking up my maintenance vitamins. Those were not tears of sadness."

Gavin held his breath so long; it was as if he would inflate into a giant blue balloon, if he didn't swoosh out an exhale. *Come on mom, I'm a big boy. What is it?* He had all kinds of thoughts creeping in his brain and they weren't good.

Gretchen McCoy paused; her lips trembled and puckered as if she was going to cry again. Then, an excited scream flew out of her fuchsia-pink lips. "Baby, your father has asked me to marry him, again! And I said yes!"

His jaw set in a deep fury. Did he just hear what he thought he just heard his mother exclaim? Gavin trained his eyes respectfully at his mother.

But, his throat clogged like a cotton ball that had been enlarged deep in his larynx. He blinked his eyes faster than a twinkling star. "Come again?" Gavin replied. Disbelief threw him off kilter. He sighed heavily and dropped his chin to his chest warily. Gretchen McCoy was oblivious to her son's body language. She had already jumped up from the cream loveseat across from where he sat in the matching armchair. His mother was beyond cloud nine; she was off the axis!

"So... you are going to renew your vows," Gavin confirmed intoned. He didn't hide his lack-luster of excitement over the news and Gretchen paused in her vigor of a prance.

"Baby? You don't seem elated of our news. What's the matter with you?" His mother frowned deeper. Gavin shrugged, unfazed. Realizing she was alone in the celebration of her elated news, Gretchen McCoy huffed audibly. She couldn't say she was puzzled by his reaction; she knew he had seen and heard them plenty of times disagreeing, but what couple didn't have their share of dark clouds? But, Gretchen pondered, he could be less perturbed by it. *Like really, baby?* Did she ask too much for her son to put aside his hang-ups and be happy for them? "I guess not," she uttered around disappointment.

"If this is what you want, mom, then I guess it's your decision to make," Gavin paused, measuring his words cautiously. "But... I respectfully have to share that I won't be happy for y'all. I just won't. I can't. And I'm sorry."

Gavin knew he spun the news to his mother that he wasn't in agreement of their renewing their vows for a loophole. He explained to his mother the best way he knew how at the time. Gavin was too conflicted by it right now. It was no reason why he should fake the funk. He'd apologized for breaking the news that he wasn't at all on board with this farce of a renewal, but he just had to keep it one hundred. It wasn't something he could get into right now. It just wasn't.

Kissing his mother's radiant, almond brown face, Gavin drew her in his taut arms for a tender hug, telling her he had somewhere he needed to go and he would call to share everything later. And, on that note, he was out of there. Gavin knew he'd better hijack it out of there before his father returned. He knew he would have lots of explaining to do but, at this point, he'd needed to make himself scarce before he made the situation worse and he'd regret it, before all hell break loose.

***

"Thank you and please come again." The young girl behind the counter cordially smiled and returned Corliss' bank card in her waiting hand.

Corliss smiled, clutching her cupcakes from Gigi's Bakery. "Thank you. Trust me, I will be back," she promised. Who can resist these delicious treats?! Corliss swiped her tongue across her lips and winked. She left the establishment with a cheerful wave and the idea that she was going to splurge on the sweets high late that evening. Gavin was not going to be a downer of her lively spirit. She invested too many times thinking of him; why did he do her the way he did? And why, that night, he looked like she spoke Bangladesh or some other foreign language? She told him it was over and he had the audacity to look like he was stunned and confused by the declaration.

That look he gave her still carved in her brain. No matter how he acted as though, he didn't know why she was throwing away what she thought was a lifetime future together; she knew better than to be persuaded by his puppy-dog face.

Corliss shook her head longingly as she settled into her car and, before pulling off, she exhaled a frustrated sigh; pressing her forehead to the steering wheel, she uttered softly, "Why God, do I allow him to get in my head? Haven't I endured too much pain in a lifetime to be buoyancy right back into the thick of things with him?" Corliss lifted pleading eyes heavenward. "Okay, Father, this is where you tell me what to do about it?"

***

Five minutes had rolled by, but it felt as though she had been traveling for thirty. She was that plagued by the circumstances that occurred earlier. She didn't need this drama and, yet, she was now in the thick middle of it all. As Corliss maneuvered in her parking space of the high-rise factory-style district, she ambled inside; her spa tub was calling her name. After splurging in the tub, she dried herself liberally, then cheerfully reached across the vanity and opened her jar of homemade essential lavender oil she'd made three days ago. Lathering her lithe body generously, minutes had passed and she pranced into her bedroom, choosing lavender silk pajamas, all the while fantasizing over the delectable treats atop of her granite countertop. It was now six thirty and she was planning to indulge in her sweet tooth with one cupcake and a nice heaping cup of organic tea, brush her teeth, and prepare for bed, since she would be arising early for her speaking engagement.

Corliss smiled affectionately at the thought of speaking to a group of girls in the nonprofit she'd started three years ago. Girls With The Green Thumbs, an organization with the objective of young girls ages 5-18 embracing their dreams and passion to the scientific career of landscaping, caring about the environment, and making an impact in a more green and recyclable world. Corliss loved nature and she loved her career as a landscaper and sponsored several landscaping camps and afterschool activities. She loved the opportunities to give back to the community. It was what made her want to apply more service learning in her career. It was her passion that she had placed on the backburner after she had broken it off with Gavin, to travel all over the world while building naturalist outdoor learning living environments for the youth. They spent many times forging out their plans to do just that together, sooner than later. But, then, that night when things turned profusely downhill.

Chapter Eight

Gavin heard the chime of his father's ringtone. He knew it would be a matter of time that he would want to have a 'little talk'. That was dandy with Gavin because he wanted to engage in a showdown, a respectable showdown, but one he planned to have with his father once and for all.

"Hello."

"Son. I need you to get yourself back over here," his dad's voice boomed angrily. "I don't know what has gotten into you, but you better recognize your behavior with your mother will not be tolerated!"

Gavin loped the sidewalk of Corliss' townhouse. He had called her and asked if he could stop by. He wanted to apologize for his behavior earlier in person. So, the confrontation with his father was not in the cards tonight. It was already after seven and Corliss had reminded him she would be turning in by nine tonight because of her speaking engagement tomorrow morning. He didn't want to disrupt her evening, but he had to make amends of what occurred earlier at the school. So, there he was allowing her to orchestrate his thoughts with noises of the present holding his attention. He didn't need hopeful feelings trying to recreate a 'new' thing between them.

Gavin blew out a resolute sigh. He knew his father would be calling, but what took him so long to get back with him? As if his father could read his mind, he explained his delay.

"Your mother told me after I had to coast it out of here just now. Hello? Are you there?"

"Yes sir. But, we will have this talk tomorrow. I called mom two hours ago and told her not to worry and that I love her and apologize for the outburst-"

"But, it doesn't explain why you feel this way!" He heard his father's roar of a clipped tone he was used to hearing when the reverend was making his demand perfectly clear.

When he was a child, it used to shutter him in absolute attention. Of course, he was not about disrespect, but he wasn't a child anymore. Gavin twisted his mouth in mockery. *Who doesn't shrivel up when his father's tone saluted in attention?* But Gavin was a grown man and his dad, with much respect, was not going to intimidate to validate.

"I have to go, sir. But, I will call you tomorrow morning and we'll set aside time to talk. I'm disconnecting now," he politely informed. "Goodbye."

Gavin heard his father disconnect without a single goodbye. Oh. He had done it now. His Pops was fire-engine furious. Gavin shrugged his right shoulder in jest, deciding he was not going to be fazed by it. "Still high and mighty," he heard himself whisper, making his way in an amble stroll. Then, he realized he was getting ready to be front and center with the love of his life for the third time today. He rang the doorbell and stepped back with nerve endings so wired, his body swayed in an unsteady gait. He held Corliss' favorite Violet Hyacinths flower clutched in his other hand, shinned in sheen of sweat. *Get a grip, man! She dumped you, remember? Kicked you to the side, for what? Or for whom?*

"Hi. I wanted to apologize. Peace offering?" He rakishly grinned. Deep dimples creased his face. Offering Corliss the vibrant plant, he grazed the tip of her fingers as she accepted and immediately felt a voltage of immense attraction in the exchange. Corliss welcomed him into her abode looking as radiant as the sun's golden rays. Her soft eyes lured him in. Her bright and cheerful smile gleamed his insides and, no matter how hard he tried to tamper down his feelings for her, that flicker always seemed to shine and he chided inwardly for allowing it to glisten.

"Thank you. I accept your apology. I was about to splurge on a cupcake. Care for one?"

Gavin chuckled, studying Corliss' sweet smile. *No sweets of the sweets could be as sweet as the woman before him...* With a crooked grin, he was tempted to share his appraisal, but voted against it. Instead, he stated the obvious sweet tooth; he knew she had when it came to cupcakes in general.

"You love your sweets, don't you? Sure." He winked. "That is, if I'm not imposing?"

Corliss cocked her head to the side; her bottom lip curled in a demure grin. "Now, you know I don't like to give up my sweets too fast. "So, yes," she nodded slowly, "I guess I can share with you?" she bantered.

Was she outright flirting? Well, they always had the jovial thing going in their relationship; nothing changed there. Corliss noticed he was still standing in the doorway of her home. "Please, have a seat." She gestured to her spacious Zen great room, with soft color pallets infused in burnt orange and cream with light and darker tones of burgundy. She had lit her aromatherapy candles of sandalwood and lavender to calm her fragile nerves seconds before, to assist in soothing her in tranquility in which she needed to ponder on what to do with this man that still had her insides tangled in a jelly of knots. Then, she glanced up at him and they shared a smile.

"Nice crib."

"Thank you. It's home," she said, biting her lips. She often engaged in the hang-up whenever she was nervous. And she was definitely nervous, but an excited nervous bubbled through her body.

She turned toward her kitchen while distracted by his alluring presence. The man always demanded a heady presence that exuded pure male. She heard his footfalls toward her loveseat. She chanced a glance as his movement in her peripheral, which treated her to a glorious view. The man was too sexy for his own good!

Shaking her head slightly, she reached into her white shaker cupboard finding a crystal vase, and then turned counter-clockwise to her farm-style sink to fill it with water. All the while, she tried mercifully to pressure down the tingle of excitement that coursed through her. He cared enough to come and check on her. *He still loves me*, she pondered. Glancing down to admire again the grape-bulb foliage, she deeply inhaled and exhaled while closing her eyes briefly; she then arranged the wiry petal flowers as a picturesque backdrop to her glass dining table. It embellished in a natural splash of a colorful centerpiece against her navy-blue walls.

A refreshing sigh blew out of her mouth before she could press her lips closed. She hadn't treated herself for a long time to a fresh bouquet of flowers since she moved in her condo. Gavin was always thoughtful in gifting her fresh ones on a frequent basis. Corliss shook her head in dismay. *No. Stop it. This was just a kind gesture. Get your head out of the swooning... he's being polite, only—apologetic for acting like a...*

"My Pops asked my mother to renew their vows," he interrupted her lingering, melancholy thoughts. "Hashtag. I'm not going to allow that to happen."

Chapter Nine

Corliss' body froze. The terseness of Gavin's words stunned her speechless. How could he not be happy for his parents? Despite what had happened in the past, Corliss could tell the couple adored one another. Gavin had to know that. The couple oozed love and appreciation the very first time Gavin introduced her. Recovering, she sauntered over to where Gavin sat with muscular arms steeped on his taut thighs. She reached out to clasp his right shoulder. She knew she shouldn't have, but it was instinctive, natural to do so. "You're troubled," she said with conviction.

Gavin sniffed. Nodding his head, he confirmed his feelings. He raked a huge hand down his 5 o'clock shadow. His broad shoulders slumped and shook visibly. Corliss moved from standing over him and took a seat next to the man she still loved deeply. He was her Boaz God designed for her. He would be her husband and she wasn't going to deny their love, their union any longer. He might be troubled, but she knew he knew trouble didn't last always. They would get through this together, for both knew the author and finisher of their faith.

Gavin was a man of faith and she knew that this too would pass. She still saw him as that strong tower; he was not perfect, only the Father held this characteristic.

As she sat next to Gavin, the closeness felt like old times. Corliss outstretched her right hand, lifting his chin upward gently. Their eyes bored in something unnamed, but Corliss knew it was more than an attraction. It was beyond that and much more. She loved this man. And she knew he felt the same.

Gavin's dark gaze drew her in to his soul. She saw the hurt, the pain that resided. There was a shimmer of tears floating in his eyes. Corliss swallowed hard. In a steady voice, "let us pray," she told him with conviction.

Gavin and Corliss stood with hands embraced, eyes closed, and heads nodded; the Holy Spirit poured out its feeding and they digested in its nourishment.

"There is a Balm in Gilead," Corliss proclaimed.

"Amen," was his only reply.

Afterwards, Corliss came to her feet, retrieved the Gigi's pastel box, and they wolfed down cupcakes after the other.

Not at all what she needed. She was only supposed to have one. But, that went out the door when she watched him lick the butter cream icing from his sexy lips. In order to stop herself from outright moaning, she wolfed down one cupcake after the other like they were going out of style!

***

"Thank you, all for coming out today..."

Corliss had Gavin and the others' rapt attention. Before leaving Corliss' condo the other night, she had extended the invitation for him to be a part of her nonprofit sponsored event taken place at the Nature Museum. Gavin immediately accepted, which surprised him because he wasn't supposed to be eager to spend more time with her, nor invest time in anything she had her hand in. He had his ulterior plan to wreak havoc on her emotionally and, yet, he was being drawn into her aura. What was it about her that made him such a softy? In the last two weeks, they were almost back into their routine, as if their break-up was just a minor setback.

Gavin blinked rapidly, realizing he had meandered off. He refocused his attention on the context of Corliss' presentation. She was presenting on research of the Green Environment. Later that afternoon, they would be touring the newly opened bird-friendly garden and the Butterfly Pavilion. The presentation explored the health benefits of urban vegetation and green space, in which Corliss had always been passionate in advocating. As she eloquently spoke of "urban greenery" and "green space", Gavin found himself conjuring in his mind how his urban design elements could be the perfect marriage. He shook his head as if he were in a smog of fog. Did he just imagine a renewal of their once relationship?

Corliss smiled brightly. The idea to invite Gavin there today was two-fold. It dawned on her the other night that this could be just the breakthrough of an icebreaker to chip away at that iceberg of pain he wrestled. So, she asked him to tag along and, surprisingly, he accepted. She called Caitlin after Gavin's visit and she gawked at the idea at first, but then gave it some real thought and finally came to terms. Not that she needed her cousin's validation, but they were a team and she valued her cousin's opinions and insights. They complimented one another well. Although she often got on her nerves, they were the yin and yang power-puffs girls! And they were going to use their energy on a certain media host. Corliss felt Gavin's gaze and it brought fission of awareness and wanton all at the same time. She stood up straighter, pushed her shoulders back, and cleared her throat. *Why was he looking at her like they were the only ones in the building? And why did she want to end this event now and take him home with her? Then what will you do?* Did Corliss really want to answer that very question?

Instead, Corliss pressed on sharing her slides of urban models and how "green infrastructure" improves an individual's physical, mental health, and overall well-being. "Statistical studies show that nature 'gone greener' results in a happier and healthier lifestyle, better health, better environment." Gavin nodded his agreement. Corliss was a wealth of knowledge and experience. And he was soaking it all in, her beauty and wit.

There was an intermission, as the girls made a bee-hive to various exhibits of the museum with families and chaperones. Gavin strolled over to Corliss, where she had just finished a conversation with an exhibitor of an insect presentation.

"Hi," he greeted with hands deep into his navy-blue Dockers trousers. Gavin acted as though he was a school-boy with a crush on the most popular and prettiest girl.

Corliss pursed her lips. She attempted to calm her jittery nerves that caused her knees to buckle. She was truly embarrassing herself now. She was a grown woman and there she was acting as though she was being approached by the handsome guy at her school locker, or somewhere. *Like really?*

She took his hand in hers. "Come on." She angled her head in the direction of the garden pergola. "Your next exercise," she supplied, when Gavin gave her the side-long glance as to ask like Arnold on the popular sitcom Different Strokes, "What you talking about, Corliss?" Several families with their children in tow were eagerly making their way out to the terrace as well. Sparks ignited and traveled up her forearm. Gavin gently latched onto Corliss' small hand, rubbing the pad of her palm lightly with his thumb. Her eyes widened in a heated attraction.

Chapter Ten

The newly grown, bird-friendly garden outside of the museum designed for the attraction of at least a hundred of birds and plants were amongst them. And Corliss' favorite bird was the Hummingbird. A flock were soaring around, nipping nectar from exotic flowers for nourishment.

"So…" Gavin pressed. The two continued the stroll amongst the chirping of birds flying freely around beautiful colorful plants strategically placed, there to attract a flock of following.

Corliss smirked; a small laugh broke the silence that had hovered. "You wanna know what do I possibly have up my sleeves?" She punched him playfully on a broad shoulder. "Am I correct?" she asked.

Gavin grinned. "Yep." He nodded. "You care to share?"

Corliss smiled and winked. "Just chill, Gav. Relax. Take deep breaths and exhale," she instructed. Her smile was like a balm of restoration.

As they toured the garden, Corliss talked about the characteristics of the Hummingbird. "You know," she said casually, "it's their nature to be very territorial. They will chase even the largest birds, such as hawks, away from their territories. They don't play that!" She laughed lightly.

Gavin peered at her. "Are you trying to draw a metaphor here?"

"I'm just saying." She shrugged her shoulders and continued her path around an array of flowers that donned the colorful garden. She kept her voice light and nonjudgmental. Her goal was not to hurdle accusations. She only wanted Gavin to see how even God's nature in creating the Hummingbird as fast breathing, fast heartbeat, and high body temperature requires that they must eat often every day, and she believed their instinctive nature to consume in such consumption, designed by God, put them in a unique situations and, yet, they come out resilient in the midst of.

Gavin nodded, knowingly. His body began to relax. He had become fixated in his parents' relationship to the point it kept him in high alert of adrenaline. He just couldn't understand why his father couldn't put down this affinity to other women. And, now, this renewing of their vows... what did his dad have up his cloak sleeves? *You won't know unless you confront the man...*

"Relax, Gavin."

Chuckling low, Gavin reached for her hand; he squeezed lightly. The two leisurely migrated through the garden, along with the other patrons who took in the sights, smells, and freedom of flight, while birds and butterflies soared in the divine plan of God's creation. He made no mistakes in how he created the natural word and its inhabitants, all designed by him for purpose.

"Thank you." He bent down to kiss her lightly on her cheek. His lips felt like feathers to her skin, like butterfly kisses.

"I didn't do anything but remind you of who is in control."

Gavin nodded. He kissed her cheek again, but his lips lingered on her face longer, causing her skin to tingle. Corliss actually felt her cheeks heat and she could imagine they were crimson and flushed by now.

Corliss stilled a second, taking in the wanton pleasure she felt by his affection. She held her breath, followed by a shallow release. *Did he just kiss me again? Oh. My!* She nodded, looking into his eyes that seared her insides in a fluttering of butterflies. They felt like they had invaded her belly— light, free, in-flight, and with purpose. *Is this the renewal of our love, our life, our purpose together?* Corliss pondered her thoughts but schooled her facial expression. She didn't want Gavin to think he was melting her insides all over again. But, he had, and she was tired of hiding the very fact the man she wanted back into her life had done just that very thing.

Chapter Eleven

The next few weeks were productive. Corliss had made purposeful strides while coaxing Gavin into exploring his inner-sanctum. They had fallen into a comfortable place, not only in the intervention exercises, but personal as well. They fed their spirit while attending her church and attending his. They also convened in bible study, either at his home or hers. The network, as Tanner confided, was impressed with the less closed-off Gavin. The producers were now feeling promising that he was turning over a newer, vibrant leaf.

Gavin and his father had begun to open up a dialogue that was making a progress—starting the healing process, the open-communication door to what had been closed off since his early years as far back as childhood.

Gavin had shared with Corliss about his father when he left her home that evening after their museum exercise. He called his father and they planned to talk after church the next day at his parents' home. Gavin had prepared to hear that his father had cheated on his mother with Ms. Wren.

And with the Vivian Armstrong topic, Gavin found out that his father was playing it low-key because he had contracted the event's planner and designer to plan he and his wife's upcoming 30th anniversary that would be at the family's church garden grounds. Gavin was stunned how much his father really wanted his mother to have a spiritual and physically beautiful renewal of their love. Then, his mother and father explained that Ms. Wren had just started teaching and that his mother was her mentor.

One day, Ms. Wren confided in his mother that she was in a domestic violence relationship. Her boyfriend, although he didn't physically abuse, he cut her deep with venom of words that ripped away bits by bits, then huge chunks of her self-esteem—emotional abuse she was going through and it was becoming worse because she had considered ending it all with her very life.

Gavin learned his mother could relate on some level. She grew up in a domestic violence home life basically her entire childhood.

When she was old enough to know what was happening, Gretchen and her father endured the emotional beating from her mother, who drank herself to death when Gretchen was fifteen and a very challenging teenager at that. She had become rebellious dealing with her mother's death, hormones, and she was going through the self-identity crisis of who she really was after hearing her mother tell her she was nothing—and would never amount to anything. Corliss couldn't phantom a mother telling her child something this horrific. She and her mother didn't agree on every life event of her life, but the one thing she knew her mother would always be was her cheerleader of support.

She and her father, who died while she was a sophomore in college, never sought out counseling and felt that a crisis should be left in the family to deal with behind closed doors. Gavin, as a young child, would hear his parents arguing over the years and he summed it to the couple leading to a breakup. But, between those closed doors and what he didn't hear, made Gavin's father, who married the love of his life, work even harder to boost her self-esteem.

His mother finally did get help and his parents both were instrumental in assisting Ms. Wren to break away from the debilitating environment and began to heal. The hug was not what he thought it was and Gavin felt like a heel. Now that he knew, Gavin admitted he could have exaggerated the hug to convey more than the naked eye could see.

Gretchen McCoy became an evangelist and the passion that blossomed within her became stronger in the ministry as she reached out to others. She had launched ministries within her community, as well as in the parish. Corliss remembered when she assisted Mrs. McCoy in one of the community block parties she had actually coordinated and implemented—that she heard still was active and just as huge today. She and evangelist McCoy had worked closely on the event. Corliss even manned the booth side by side with her in bible trivia. She absolutely adored her and the lively side of Mrs. McCoy back then, and Corliss remembered that day as the moment she knew Gretchen McCoy was a powerful and instrumental vehicle in the ministry.

She could see why Mrs. Olmstead, as she opened up to her last week, had a spirit of discernment that drew her in to her presence. And the way she put her creative twist on the games back in the day, that really gave the youth the interest and the desire to know the word in a fun and, yet, profound in applying to their young lives. Corliss always felt it was an awe experience, and she was truly blessed to be a part of her ministry. Corliss was glad she was able to witness that side of Mrs. McCoy. Their closeness grew over the years but, then, that night…

Gavin never knew any of this. He now felt like if he had known why his parents took such a passion in being there for others, he would have not felt pressured to believe he was from a broken home where his father was creeping out on his marriage. He kept that proverbial chip on his shoulder and allowed it to keep him from freely and fully opening up to her.

"Hey, what's taking you so long, girl? Hello? I'm waiting for that cool, refreshing drink," he taunted.

Corliss smiled. A warm tingle surged deep in her gut. "I'm coming, man..." she chortled in a raspy chuckle, as she busied herself in preparing their frothy drinks. Gavin loved her lemon balm iced tea and said it was the best, ever! Well, she didn't know about that, but she did pride herself in creating the cool refreshing beverage and, as the first week of summer offered its sweltering spread of sauntering heat, the pleasure of soaking down chocolate-chips with their cool beverage was like old times; it was the perfect anecdotal memory she'd always embraced and nestled in her mind over the years.

They hadn't engaged in what happened that night she decided to end their romance; that day would come, Corliss believed. She was just intent in Gavin sorting out his emotions—those barriers that kept him imprisoned in his head and, as a result, his well-being took the brunt of it all.

After engaging in the decadent cookies and drink, Corliss got to business in sharing with Gavin of their next exercise. But, as she learned, Gavin had other motives. Drawing her from the loveseat onto her bare feet, he pressed their bodies together and dipped his dark head while angled in on her lips.

Corliss' breath stalled in her chest. A whispering of faint breaths whipped from her lips. *He's going to kiss me... and I want him to...*

Gavin took his time exploring the crevices of her mouth. She tasted like the minty treats they just devoured and he moaned at the way her mouth still drew him in. He bathed his tongued with hers, stroke by stroke; Gavin was renewing his craven for her; he was falling hard for those succulent lips. Oh, how he missed this. How was he going to stop himself from wanting more?

Gavin took Corliss' right wrist in one fluid, gentle twirl, her back now fused against his heated body. His head dipped and molten-lava tongue slid languidly across her neck, journeying to the exposed skin below her collarbone. He could never get enough of her scent. Today, she was wearing a fruity fragrance. It teased his senses and his loins rose to attention. A mixture of lust and passion singed through his body. After all, he was human, so it was natural for his body to react to her in this way; he wasn't dead. He was alive! But, man, he was trying to quench the fire that Corliss had lit.

Gavin's nostrils flared. He groaned deep in his chest, peppering her flesh with soft kisses. He was tempted to journey below... instead, he inhaled in the pear scent she wore, doing all kinds of crazy things to his head and below. "Hmmm. You smell so good. Delicious in fact," he huskily shared. "Let's finished this in the…" Screech. Replay…

Gavin's words froze in his throat. He wanted a replay because he knew the vise of temptation was coiling big-time in his brain and below.

But, not before he knew she heard the raw lust in his timbre. He was a man and, despite how he tried to stay pure, he wanted Corliss in ways he knew would stray him if he didn't get out of her place!

Corliss' eyelids lazily fluttered to a close in a sensuous haze. Her body was on fire. *Hold up... wait a minute,* her conscience cautioned. A flash of awareness popped her eyes wide. She slowly drew back from his body while turning to him, touching his succulent lip with a rose-petal pink finger; she shook her head reluctantly, but she knew she had to stay affirmed. "You see, my answer remains the same—and that's a no. Not until. Well…" She shrugged flippantly and chuckled lightly. "That's really three answers, for you, McCoy. But, I tell you…" She shook her head and then patted her face that was now damp. *There you go girl… put a lid on that… He's preparing you… for greater.*

She blew out a laborious sigh. "Whew!" she uttered, draping a hand down the curvy column of her shoulder. "You know how Jill Scott asked in Tyler Perry's Why Did I Get Married? Well… um. Can we pray?"

"Bur…" Gavin blew out. His body trembling like he had been doused with a bucket of ice. "Yeah, sweetheart, that's an excellent idea. I believe we should get to praying, like pronto," he solemnly admitted.

Chapter Twelve

"Whoa. Slow your roll, man. Back up a sec. What's that again?" Tanner asked.

Gavin rolled his eyes. "Man, you heard me! Stop fronting."

Tanner let out an amused laugh. "So... you couldn't resist the woman. What was all that about send her away, talk to you when trying to sell?" Tanner mimicked in the tone that Gavin used that day he had come into town to deliver the news to Gavin. Tanner had decided he would cruise into Charlotte, deliver the news to his homeboy, and visit his parents while he had a few days available, before his publicity duties had him across cities from Atlanta and L.A.

He had hoped he would also be able to see the gorgeous Caitlin while he was in town but, with Gavin and his antics and his parents planning his entire weekend there, he didn't get the chance. But, trust, Tanner was very much so interested in spending some time with her in the near future. And now that her cousin and his best friend were hooking up, would he seize the opportunity if it presented itself?

"Hey. What's up Tanner?"

Tanner shook off the uncomfortable thoughts. He realized Gavin was still on the other line and that he had just gone rogue. He was slipping; Caitlin and his connection to her would have to be put on the back-burner. He was too busy, anyway, to start something with her. He was all about his business and that's how it should stay.

"Uh. What did you say?"

"Where did you go, man?" Gavin asked in amusement.

Tanner pushed up on his forearms of his recliner and frowned. "I'm here, man."

Gavin chuckled. "Right... you're thinking about a certain cousin of Corliss'? Am I right?"

"You're deflecting, man. It's about you and Corliss. So, are you going to let that go and start anew?"

Gavin blew out a defeated sigh. "You got me," he admitted. "Now, tell me what am I going to do? I need her to open up on why she ended things in the first place?"

"Uh-uh. I'm not getting in the middle of that, man! You all need to address that elephant in the room when you both know it's time to come correct."

Gavin sighed heavily. He knew this to be true. They had to get out there. The tiptoeing around the bush had to come to a screeching halt if they were going to do this again. "Well, you should be getting your invitation soon to my parents' renewing their vows in the next two months," Gavin said, changing the subject. He would have to cross that bridge when it came around.

"Again. Congratulations on that!" Tanner remarked in a cheerful acknowledgment. "Those two deserve it!"

Gavin bopped his head excitedly, in agreement of his friend's accolade. His pops was not perfect, but Gavin had discovered he never gave him the benefit of the doubt all these years. A misunderstanding had drawn a wedge between them silently but evident in the tension that was fabricated in his mind. Now that he knew the truth, they could begin to mend that fence and rebuild the father and son's bond.

"Okay. That's my cue."

"Your cue for what, man?" Gavin asked as a rebuttal. He knew it was coming. Tanner was about to lay it on him. It was no escaping it. And, then, he had to ask. Man, when was he going to learn this brother knew him like a biological brother, the one he never had but, if he had one, Tanner would be the epitome of the perfect sibling. Sure. They had their differences and didn't often see eye-to-eye, but it was all about brotherly love. They had each other's back and, despite Gavin being a stubborn man to the umpteenth degree, he knew Tanner only wanted the best for him—and vice versa.

"Flipping my publicist hat on; don't forget you want a syndication of *Gavin Makes House Calls*, so keep your eye on the prize!"

Gavin quirked a dark eyebrow. "Oh yeah. Uh... I've been meaning to run something by you. About that..."

"Do I want to even know, man? I'm afraid to ask," Tanner sighed in a long breath. "What was it that you meant to run by me?"

"I've been pondering-,"

"Spill it. Gav. Let me have the short version."

"What do you think about enhancing the show; you know, shake things up a bit?"

"Tan. Man, where you at?"

"Gavin-"

"Just hear me out, man. This is what I'm proposing..."

***

Corliss wrung her sweaty palms nervously in a tight squeeze. She couldn't believe she was acting as if this was her first 'real' date with Gavin. But, in hindsight, it really was after all that had happened since that night she'd broken things off. Was this a fresh start? Corliss' eyes closed then opened wide-eyed, as she took in several deep breaths and blew out audibly. There she was getting ahead of herself. Even her mother suggested she take things slow where Gavin was concerned.

She had consulted with the matriarch twice about where things were heading with Gavin. Her mother and father, Malachi Adams, now resided on Hilton Head Island. They had retired early from their professions as school administrators four years ago and were enjoying their retirement to the fullest. Corliss was happy for them; their marriage hadn't always been 'peaches and cream' her mother shared, but marriage was like a job; you had to be willing to do the work to reap the pay off. But, her mother had always told her to seek God's guidance in every actions and decisions she made and, this, whatever it was leading to with Gavin, was definitely a wise precursor.

She couldn't afford to just get 'caught' up in the nostalgic feelings. She was not that young and giddy college student experiencing adulthood with vulnerabilities surmounting her in the physical realm. Yes. She was very physically attracted to Gavin but, this time, it was so much more; she wanted to reconnect on a more spiritual plateau.

A week later on a golden, panoramic Friday afternoon and Gavin was taking her to the Daniel Stowe's Botanical Garden for the Sip and Stroll event later that evening. Corliss bit into her bottom lip, glancing a perusal of her casual summer time outfit in the full-length vanity mirror. Bringing a jittery hand down her chevron strap shift dress, Corliss creased out the imaginary wrinkles. She wanted to look perfect for Gavin. Encased on her petite feet were light tan, laced-up booties and she voted for a straw, tan color floppy hat. Taking a cursory glimpse at her reflection, she drew a small smile of approval and prodded her way to the great room to wait for her handsome date.

***

Corliss knew the time was winding down for this assignment. She had made sufficient progress in enhancing Gavin's outlook on the personal and now it was on to the business side, in which she felt he had already begun to balance the two. He had made progress and steps to change that she knew was going to heighten his career. She knelt on her knees and steeped her hands with her head bowed; she prayed diligently in the midst of her great room for the Holy Spirit on Gavin's behalf.

Her doorbell chimed just as she completed her prayer, and she strolled to answer and was greeted with a handsome, wide grin. He was smiling down at her. And Corliss couldn't help to feel a promising spirit flow through her brain. *I love this man... but God loves him even more... it's His Will, not mine, of what all He has for Gavin McCoy!*

"Hi, gorgeous."

"Hey," she answered. She hoped she didn't sound breathless by his sexy timbre.

Just as soon as she welcomed him in, Gavin swooped her in his arms and kissed her passionately, leaving her dizzy induced by his forwardness.

"Wow..." Corliss could only utter.

"Wow, is right," he told her. "I want us back!"

***

Daniel Stowe's Botanical Garden, the epitome of reconnecting with nature, was what had Corliss super excited; although, she was an active member and would find herself there at least once a year, it was still her passion to be amongst the visitors enjoying the splendor of God's creation. Located within 380 acres on the banks of Lake Wylie, there was such a variety of nature-inspired jewels to explore. From beautiful and spectacular gardens, sparkling fountains, a conservatory dedicated to nature's finest from tropical plants, orchids, and a pavilion along with a garden store and hilly, greens nature trails awaiting visitors who loved nature, just as Corliss and Gavin.

It was Sip and Stroll night, and the couple would be engaging in a stroll in the golden hew of the summer's warmth garnish light, while exploring gorgeous buds of the season. The last time they visited together, it was a weekend trip over six years ago. It had been awhile, but they were there together now, and that's what really mattered to Corliss. Was there a certain reason why he chose this setting—this place at this time of their renewal?

"This is nice," Gavin acknowledged and smiled at her, as he twisted his body in his seat of one of the many benches that adorned the garden pavilion. They had strolled along the cobblestone pathway, admiring the rainbow of colored flowers and taking in the scenic visuals along the way, as they sipped on their cucumber mint sparkler. The refreshing beverage was light and tangy and ushered tranquility and a peaceful mood that both Gavin and Corliss agreed was just the backdrop to opening the dialogue they knew needed to be put out there.

"So... beautiful," Gavin prodded. He cleared his throat. Man! He didn't think he would be this nervous to explain himself. He didn't know why he hadn't done anything wrong for her not to have trusted him. Or had he?

Corliss softly smiled and embraced her small hands into Gavin's. "Are you ready to have this talk here?" She glanced around briefly before her gaze found his again. "Are you sure this is the time?"

Gavin's expression told her he wasn't too certain. Did that mean she was right about what she expected that night? She was told he was forgoing the promise they made to stay pure and he'd already had a prospect waiting to relieve him from the hiatus. Reliving those words she was told by one of their closest friends still cut her raw, like a sharp spear cutting her insides in slices, chunks by chunks. But, she wasn't going to show him that side again. Yes. She loved him and was not denying it but, still, there were reservations of how much she could still display. And she wasn't going to be the sitting duck waiting for him to return to explain why he made her cry out her soul that vivid night imprinted in her working memory.

But, Corliss knew she couldn't geek out now, so she straightened her back and prepared to hear the words, despite the results they would render. It was time. Long overdue. *Yes, it's time... no reason to delay,* she meandered in fragile thoughts. She told herself, no matter the case may be, she was not going to let it interfere with their professional relationship. She would continue to be his advocate—no matter what...

"About that night, Corliss..."

Here it comes...

Corliss flinched inwardly. She prayed that her outward appearance didn't show how badly she was clinging to every syllable. Her knees were buckling now and she chided for her body to stop its haywire reaction.

"Corliss?" She heard him call out her name. Where had she gone? Corliss blinked. She shook away the fog.

"Yes," she trained a focus gaze, "please continue."

"I love you. And that night... the night I was going to pour out my soul to you, you ended things. And the fact of the matter, I should have fought for us—our love. But, I was too stubborn. I didn't want to beg," Gavin paused as he waited for a couple who was leisurely taking their time along the pathway where they sat. "I... feared of being rejected," he continued once the path was clear of hearing distance. *Maybe this wasn't the place after all to get into this...*

"Go ahead, sweetheart... it's okay." Corliss flitted a cursory glance around the pavilion. "I'm listening," she soothingly coasted.

Gavin nodded knowingly. He swallowed hard. "I-I don't understand why you ended things. Why, Corliss? I think... no, I *deserve* an explanation once and for all."

Corliss nodded, while squeezing his hands. Lord knows she needed the prodding to continue on. This was it. She was going to be straight up honest with him. No more hiding behind the veil. "Yes. You do. I was told by a mutual friend that she overheard a conversation you were having with one of your frat brothers. That... that you were getting tired of waiting for me, for us, to be together sexually again. I- I then saw you that same night, hugging a knock-out of a beauty outside of the student union."

"Wait." Gavin dropped her hands as he brought a hand beneath her chin. He gently lifted it, seeing the droplets of tears pooling her eyes and trickling down the sides of her smooth cream face. Something in Gavin's heart ebbed a stinging feeling to censor her tears. "Please don't cry," Gavin soothed, caressing the pad of his thumb to wipe away the tears that were flowing heavily. "Listen, sweetheart. Please beautiful, don't cry. That conversation did happen, but I was being honest. I'm not going to lie and tell you it wasn't hard to resist you. It was a temptation. I will not say that it was easy to refrain. But, sweetheart, I did not cheat on you that night or any morning, day, or night. Who you saw that evening was my cousin, Stephanie."

"Your cousin in Los Angeles," Corliss replied. A knowing expression dawned on her face. She remembered Gavin mentioning her. He was fondly proud of his youngest cousin. She was like the baby sister he'd never had. Gavin was the only child, just as she was the only child. That was one of the many things they had in common. And, yet, there were many associations that they shared by affiliation back then. Corliss realized she was allowing her brain to zone out. She was relieved to know now that he hadn't stepped out on her. She exhaled a breath of relief.

Her name immediately brought back a memory base now. But, then, like Corliss was catapulted back to that phase in their lives, she shook her head in disbelief that there was more to it. "But still, Gavin," she pressed on. She had to let him know how deeply hurt she was and, even now, when he disconnected, cutting off his feelings from her. "You had this isolation thing going on for like two weeks and you wouldn't open up to me."

"And, for that, I apologize, dear heart. It wasn't because I didn't want us to not be. Please know that was far beyond the case," Gavin explained. "I was hurting. And I shouldn't have taken it out on you. I was just ego tripping. You know. My frats were teasing about it." He let out a short laugh before continuing; "I allowed it to put a seed of discord between us. I love you. And I want us back, do you hear me?"

Corliss nodded, wiping at her now red eyes. She sniffed and finally nodded a sincere understand. She was feeling like things were actually going to be okay again. She gifted him a smile of affirmation. "And, I love you too."

Gavin smiled. "Thank God." And they leaned into one another's mouth in a chaste but soulful kiss. No words were uttered. Corliss could hear her heart thumping loudly in her chest amongst the solitude of her mind. She and Gavin may be surrounded by throngs of people amidst but, right there, right now, it was as if they were transported to a secret place where their hearts interwoven in a God's cupid of approval. Gavin and Corliss shared another passionate kiss; this time, it had Corliss' feet upturned. The couple sealed with a clinking toast to their renewed future. Gavin and

Corliss finished off their drinks and sprinted across the lawn to grab nachos from one of the food trucks parked—a favorite snack of theirs because that's what the two decided to nibble on during their first date.

**

Two weeks later, Gavin was all about "making it do what it do, God's style". After much prayer, supplication, and discussions with Tanner, his parents and, of course, Corliss, Gavin knew what he wanted to do. Corliss was in support of him and he knew this woman was for him and not against him.

"So, man, you know this is a game changer," Tanner told him as they were playing a game of one-on-one basketball in their church's gym after men's bible study. Tanner was back in the Queen city and knew he needed to make the study, after being pulled here and there in business deals.

"Yep," Gavin gingerly answered, shooting a three-pointer with his hands still in the 'in your face' salute. "This man," he countered, "is what I've been asking the Lord to direct me in the path he has for me. It's been a stirring and I've been hearing the call but not hearkening to it. I'm going to let go of the playing it too safely and trust in Him and his faithfulness!"

"Amen!" Tanner cheered, receiving the ball from Gavin. He boldly drove it to the net, followed by a mean slam dunk.

"Let's get to work marketing my new brand, son!"

"I'm on it like yesterday, man! I've got this," Tanner replied.

"As you should be, because it's going to be paramount!"

"Oh, yeah?" Tanner chuckled.

"Word," Gavin remarked, accepting the ball from his homeboy. Driving to the net with a confident swagger, he followed in a resounding dunk. "Amen style," he added in a grin while glancing over his shoulder at Tanner.

"Amen." Tanner grinned back and the two men played another round before calling it quits to jump in the shower. Tanner had work to mull over and Gavin was meeting his now fiancée, and he couldn't wait to see her and share his elated news of the network.

Chapter Thirteen

After washing up, Gavin met his queen at their weekly dinner engagement. He could barely hold back the excitement that was brewing his insides. He felt lighter now, like the weight of the world had been lifted off his shoulders. Gavin could admit the boulder brought a damper in his attitude and spirit, but it taught him life skills with the assistance of his soulmate, Corliss Valencia Adams. But it was the intervention and his first priority, the Lord and Savior, Jesus Christ, who deserved all the praises. And, for that, he knew he could walk into his season with faithfulness and obedience until him!

As Donald Lawrence's song reminded him of being confident in his passionate career turn, Gavin waltzed into the dining area of BlueNotes, a New Orleans jazz and blues bar in the prominent University area. "Walk into your season," he hummed the chorus in a jovial tune and swag in his stroll. He was quickly greeted by a hostess. It was the theme of his new beginning. And he was going to make it do what it do, putting his best foot forward.

"Well, hello there, again Gavin." Morgan, a member of his church, cordially ushered him into the soulful lounge of florescent hues of purple, gold, and deep burgundy decorum. Morgan warmly smiled. "Right this way…"

"A certain lovely lady is waiting." She winked, leading him to his soon-to-be bride and the mother of his children.

"Thank you, and Hello Morgan," Gavin nodded. "Please lead the way," he told her as the song, Season, continued to laden in his Spirit.

As he sauntered in step behind Morgan, he began singing in declaration, "I know that you invested a lot, but the return has been slow. You throw up your hands and say, I give up. I just can't take it anymore, but I hear the Spirit say that it's your time, the wait is over, walk into your season…"

Epilogue

Three Years Later…

"I now pronounce you the blessed founders of Restoration, Inc. You may lift your garden tools."

Gavin and Corliss McCoy smiled and gazed lovingly in each other's eyes proudly, sealing the blessing with a tender kiss.

"We did it, babe!" Gavin whispered for her ears only. My bad." He pounded his chest in a fist and lifted a humbling gaze heavenward.

"Mommy… Daddy!" The couple's three-year old daughter's high-pitch voice shrilled in excitement. Corlissa Angelica sprinted toward her parents; her twin brother, Gavin Owen Jr., following in her fleeting footsteps; well, rather trying to keep up in pace with his older sister by three minutes.

"Slow down, where is the fire?" he asked, nearly out of breath. Corliss and Gavin chuckled in unison.

The twins were quite the animated characters. Gavin Jr. had recently taken on mimicking his dad's words, Corliss thought. How many times had Gavin Sr. had to warn their twins to slow down and smell the roses in the last two years of their youthful lives? Ever since they were able to toddle around, Corliss and Gavin had always advocated and nurtured in their ball of energetic daughter and son the passion of nature's aesthetic and outdoor learning and healthy practices.

"You're gonna be a track star!" he told his sister. Corlissa glanced briefly over her shoulder, giving him a wide smile while she shrugged her shoulder and giggled.

"Catch up, slow poke!"

"Now, Corlissa. Stop teasing your brother."

"O…k…" Her chestnut brown face morphed into a slight frown. "But mommy, you always tell me I can be con-con…"

"Confident," Gavin gently, and with patience, supplied the word his beautiful and intelligent daughter tried conveying. He bent down to gather her playfully in his arms and turned her upside down.

"Daddy!" Corlissa screamed playfully. Her gregarious laughter always brought a lighter side into his heart and nestled his spirits. Despite the daunting task of events that had occurred over the last two years: resigning with the network, but in a new segment where he and his wife teamed up to bring outdoor experiences on a more creative, physical, social, and emotional well-being for young children, traveling, and restoring playgrounds as youth ministers in missions for their church, was just as impactful and fulfilling. Restoration Inc. was their new foundation of a youth enrichment center geared to nurture the mind and soul of the youth, one designer, landscape scientist, and two mommy and daddy helpers, one garden, one enchanting forest at a time…

THE END

About The Author

Tonya is a native of Charlotte, North Carolina where she continues to live. Renewal to Passion is her debut inspirational/contemporary novella. She... knew she always wanted to become an author, someday. She penned her first manuscript at the age of sixteen and has written ever since.

Tonya enjoys creating stories about life and its supporting cast centered on romantic elements, heroes and heroines that are complex and pay homage to her vivid imagination. A true and wholesome love story pulls at her heartstrings—as she is an avid, romantic at heart.

She is an enthusiast couch potato whenever it comes to The Hallmark Channel. She also enjoys watching Home and Garden, TV in which she loves to design creative spaces in her designer's hat, imagination, of course!

She enjoys spending quality time with her loving and supportive family and treasures the moments of bible study and family devotion with her husband, Mitchell, and sons Kendall and Cameron taking time out of their busy schedules over the years, focusing on God's blessings, guidance, unchanging grace, mercy and faithfulness in their lives. These dedicated moments are coined as 'Family Prayer.'

77771883R00041

Made in the USA
Columbia, SC
27 September 2017